Letters to the Baumgartners

By Selena Kitt

eXcessica publishing

Letters to the Baumgartners © 2011 by Selena Kitt

Excessica LLC
486 S. Ripley #164
Alpena MI 49707

To order additional copies of this book, contact:
books@excessica.com
www.excessica.com

Cover art © 2015 Taria Reed
First Edition December 2011

Chapter One

Dear Carrie and Doc,

I cannot believe Janie is turning a year old in March! How is it even possible? I know you were so worried when she was born two months early—we all were—such a tiny baby in an incubator with all those tubes and feeds. Poor girl. But look at her now! The pictures you sent are tacked to a bulletin board in my little room at Cara Lucia's. She exclaims over Janie's picture every time she sees it—and inevitably asks me, "When are you getting married and having babies?" She either wants to feed you or marry you off. Of course, every old Italian woman in Venice seems to have the same goals for the younger ones. It's all about unione e bambini!

And yes, I've told her about Mason. And Isabella.

In spite of what everyone seems to think, I didn't come here to run away. You bring your problems with you anyway, right? That's what they say. But I have no interest in marriage again, and having children seems like a distant dream.

But you guys, I can't tell you how glad I am that you have little Janie. You look so happy in the photos, I could just burst. I hope Janie has an amazing first birthday and she likes my gift. Cara Lucia made it, in case you thought I'd turned domestic or something. Isn't it beautiful? She'll look like an angel in it, I know. Send pictures! The women here can weave and knit faster than they can shear the sheep!

I wish I could be there! In three more months, my student exchange will be up, and I'll be looking for a job, most likely back in the states, unless I can get my visa extended. Maybe I can find something in

Michigan, near you guys? Although the thought of being so close to Mason again makes my stomach go all fluttery. Is it wrong for me to miss him still? It's not that I doubt my decision. He was clearly not ready to be a grown-up and have a grown-up relationship, and between his mother issues and his refusal to accept or support my coming to Italy, I know I did the right thing.

But I loved him, and I still miss him.

And I miss you guys too. So much. More than I could ever say. Even if I'm not interested in finding any long-term sort of relationship right now, I have to admit, I'm a little lonely. It's just me and Jezebel against the world—and while I love my kitty and she's great at keeping me warm at night, there's still something missing...

No one but tourists traveled in gondolas.

I wouldn't have set foot in one under normal circumstances but I'd missed the water-bus and there wasn't a water-taxi in sight—they were all down near the Grand Canal waiting to take tourists from Carnavale to their dinner reservations after the festivities.

I was desperate when I approached the gondolier who would change my life. He was stretched out in his gondola, which was tied to a post, wearing the usual gondolier uniform—a black and white horizontally striped long-sleeved shirt. It wasn't warm, so he had a black down vest on over that, but the requisite flat, wide brimmed straw hat with a red sash tied around it was propped over his face against a dreary mid-day Italian drizzle. To me, he looked like an Amish referee.

I didn't even warn him—I just stepped into the boat, kicking his calf as I took a seat to wake him up.

"Eighty euro for forty minutes." He spoke English in a thick Italian accent, but he didn't move from his reclined position.

"No need to give me the usual tourist crap." My Italian was nearly perfect and the gondolier grunted fully awake, peering out at me from under the brim of his hat, his eyes hidden in shadow. "I just need a ride."

"Where to?" He spoke Italian with me now that it was clear I wasn't a tourist. "This isn't a taxi."

"If you hadn't noticed, there aren't any." I waved my hand toward the empty waterway. Practically everyone was down at the Piazza San Marco, enjoying the very last day of a two-week Carnavale celebration. I, for one, was glad it was finally over.

"What's so important it can't wait?" he inquired, but he was already untying the gondola and pushing off. The initial rocking motion always made me momentarily woozy and I clutched the sides of the boat.

"I just need to post something." I patted my bag where both letter and package waited. The Italian mail service was unreliable and slow, and I'd already waited too long to send it because Cara Lucia insisted on adding a knitted cap to go with the sweater she'd made. It had to get to the states in time for my little goddaughter's birthday just three weeks away.

"So you don't want the usual tour?" He spoke casual Italian with me and I smiled inwardly, proud. I'd been studying the language for years, but it had taken my immersion into the lifestyle and culture to really make me fluent. With my dark hair and eyes, I could probably pass for Italian, rather than the Midwest white bread mongrel breed I really was.

"No, *grazie.*" I huddled at the end of the gondola, wishing for the canopy of a water-taxi. The weather was more mist than rain. February in Italy was capricious. It could rain, or snow, or be sunny—all in one day.

I grabbed the sides of the boat as the gondolier reached under one of the seats, making the gondola rock gently as we slid through the water. I should have been used to all the jostling after living in Venice for eight months, but the fact that every time I wanted to travel anywhere, I had to use a mode of transportation that required me to move off of solid land, still made me nervous.

"*Siete freddi,*" he said, handing me a blanket. It was knitted—probably by his Italian mother or aunt, I guessed—quite beautiful, in fact.

"No, I'm not cold," I lied, continuing in Italian, trying not to let my teeth clatter together.

The gondolier raised an eyebrow but didn't call me on my bluff, putting the blanket down on the seat in front of me, taking a step back and then hopping up onto the front edge of the gondola. The whole boat tilted with the motion and I gasped, clutching the sides, gritting my teeth as he used his long pole, back and forth, to steer us through the current.

"Be careful up there!" I remarked, watching as he took a wide stance, balanced at the very end of the gondola. I never understood how they could do that.

"This isn't the city for a woman afraid of water," he remarked, grinning when I rolled my eyes in his direction. He was the youngest gondolier I'd ever seen, probably my age, his dark hair curling under the lip of his hat, his full lips parted in a smile.

"I'm not afraid of water," I protested. "I just... don't like it."

"Like a cat." He laughed. "You can swim, but you'd rather not?"

"Something like that."

"A pretty girl like you should be down in the Piazza, dressed up for Carnavale."

I rolled my eyes and tried to make myself smaller against the other side of the gondola. "I don't like parties either."

"What do you like?"

I glared at him. "Gondoliers who mind their own business."

He staggered, his hand over his heart, groaning as if he were in a great deal of pain. The dramatic gesture made the boat rock and I gasped, hanging on.

"Hey!" I protested. "Don't do that!"

"You break-a my heart." He said this in English, like a typical Italian, and it made me laugh out loud in spite of myself. His switch back to Italian made my stomach flutter. Hearing the language spoken— especially by someone decidedly tall, dark and handsome—still made me kind of swoon a little. "That's better. You're a true beauty when you smile."

"Flattery will get you nowhere." So I lied.

"What will get me somewhere?" The mischievous glint in his eyes made my stomach do another little flip. There were plenty of men in Italy, some of them very nice-looking, all of them, young and old, flirtatious and outgoing—but so far, I'd stayed immune to charm of Italian men. Mostly by sheer will, I had to admit.

"Not rocking the boat," I retorted, sticking my tongue out at him.

He laughed, shifting his hip, making the gondola see-saw on the water. "Ah, but I like to 'rock the boat.' Isn't that what you Americans say?"

I frowned. "How did you know I was American?"

"I didn't." His grin stretched ear-to-ear. "But I do now."

I couldn't help smiling at him. "That wasn't very nice."

"I'm not a nice man." His eyebrows knitted and he scowled in my direction. "In fact, I'm a very bad, bad man."

"I don't believe you."

Then that bright smile was back again. "But don't American women like 'bad boys?'"

"Where did you hear that?"

"American television of course."

I snorted. "Of course."

"So it's not true?"

"Oh it's true." I nodded sagely. "All American woman like bad boys. And men in uniforms. And men with big bank accounts. And great big..."

I let my sentence trail off, looking sideways at him.

"Well one out of four isn't bad, eh?" He shrugged, using his long pole—*no metaphor there,* I thought wryly—to steer us through the waterways of Venice.

"Are you going to make me guess which one?" I teased. I knew I was flirting with him, encouraging him, in fact. What was wrong with me today?

"No, I would never make you guess." He met my eyes, his look quite serious. I felt my cheeks flush and was glad for the chill in the air. The rain had finally stopped, and although the water was choppy, it reflected a bit of hazy sun trying to make its way through the clouds.

"So what are you doing here in Italia, Americano?" He changed the subject as smoothly as he navigated his boat through the water.

"I'm in an exchange program. Studying Italian."

"Of course." He nodded, as if he'd guessed. He probably had—there were plenty of foreign exchange students in Italy, although most were undergraduates, still in their college partying days, spending long hours drinking wine in the cafés during the day when they weren't in class and dancing at clubs into the wee hours of the night. I was a graduate student, far more serious about my studies and the time I spent in Italy, since I had to finish my thesis in just one year.

"Do you need a study partner?" he asked, flirting again.

I didn't rebuff him. "Are you offering your services?"

"In any way I can assist you." He swept his hat off his head and bowed low. His balance up there on the edge of the gondola took my breath away.

"Do you think I need practice?" I protested.

"Your Italian is good," he admitted. "But practice makes perfect, eh? Isn't that what Americans say?"

"Oh look, yet another masked man." I pointed toward the shore where someone was dressed up in costume. They were everywhere I turned this week, men, women and children all made up in masks and feathers, satin and lace. "I feel like I'm in an episode of *The Lone Ranger*."

The Italian blinked at me. "The Lone...what?"

"I thought you watched American TV." I smiled. "It's an old television show."

"How can you come to Italy and not attend Carnavale?" He looked genuinely puzzled by my lack of interest.

"It's just a big Mardi Gras, right?" I shrugged. "You've seen one, you've seen them all."

"There is nothing like Carnavale!" the Italian man protested.

"Yes there is. We celebrate it in New Orleans just like you do here. Parades and costumes. Well, we're a little more crude about it I guess. Women flash their breasts for some beads and baubles. Typical Americans, eh?"

"I like this custom." He grinned.

"I'm not religious," I admitted. "So I don't give up anything for Lent or do much on Fat Tuesday."

"Not Catholic?"

I shook my head.

"My mother is crossing herself and saying a prayer for you right now." He winked. "So what do you Americans do on this 'Fat Tuesday?'"

"Well, in America, mostly people go to work and eat Paczkis."

"Paczkis. Aren't those Polish donuts?"

"Indeed they are," I agreed. "About five hundred calories a piece."

He smirked. "Sounds delightful."

"Now you start to understand why I'm in Italy instead of the states."

"But you're not at Carnavale!"

I glanced up at him, shading my eyes, the sun finally making a full appearance. "Neither are you."

"Ah, true, but a man has to earn his bread."

I looked around the empty canal. There were a few boats docked and some people on the streets, but most of them were at the Piazza. "You do a lot of gondola rides during Carnavale?"

"Yes, it's our busiest week in the winter, although I thought about taking today off and attending the festivities. The last day of Carnavale is always the grandest." He smiled down at me. "But now I'm glad I didn't."

"Do you own your own boat?" I asked, trying to change the subject, nowhere near as smooth as he was. Going to post a letter usually took me ten minutes via the waterways, tops, but taking a gondola was slowing down the whole process considerably.

"I do," he said. "My boat, my business. I like to be in control."

My breath went away at his words, my mouth dry. I looked away from him, not able to meet his gaze, grabbing the blanket he'd left and pulling it over my knees.

"I think the whole Carnavale thing is overrated. It's all for tourists." I made another attempt to steer the conversation elsewhere. "It's been costumes everywhere I go for the past two weeks. Too much noise, too many crowds."

"Ah, but bella, the food alone is worth the crowds on the streets!" His eyes rolled back and he rubbed his belly, smacking his lips as if he could taste some delicacy on his tongue. Italians were always so overly demonstrative—that was one stereotype that had proved to be true.

"Is it good?" I found myself thinking of the bread, cheese and fruit I had left for dinner back at my flat.

"Good?" His eyes snapped open and he threw his arms wide, nearly losing his pole. "Mio Dio! It's to die for! Isn't that what you Americans say when it's too good for words?"

I smiled. "Yes, that's what we Americans say."

"You should come to dinner with me at least." He concentrated now on steering the long boat down another narrow canal—we were almost to the post office.

I quickly made excuses. "Oh, I really don't feel like going out, not with all the people..."

"Not out." He slowed the boat using his long pole. "To my home. Come see how we really do Shrove Tuesday in Venice. You'll leave so full I'll have to carry you home."

"Is that your evil plan, bad boy?" I teased as the gondola came to a stop. He used a rope around a post to pull the boat in closer to the shore.

He laughed. "Yes, that's my evil plan. Are you a willing victim?"

"I don't even know your name," I reminded him.

"Nico Bianchi." He held out his hand and I shook it, feeling the warm press of his palm against mine.

"Dani," I replied. "Danielle Stuart."

He nodded, satisfied. "See, now we are not strangers."

"Let me think about it." I accepted his help onto shore, glancing up at him. He looked so hopeful—but I knew I shouldn't. Cara Lucia had invited me to her family's Carnavale celebration but I had begged off, planning to just snuggle up with Jezebel and read the whole day away. "I need to post this before they shut their doors."

It was nearly noon, and I barely made it in before they closed for the holiday. The postal workers were all in costume, chatting about Carnavale. They were headed down to the Piazza as soon as they were done and seemed annoyed to have to deal with my little package, but I was glad I'd made it.

I glanced out the window and saw the gondolier chatting with another man, a little bit older, not in costume. He was wearing a suit and carrying a briefcase, a strange sight during Carnavale, when masks and make-up were the norm.

The men laughed together and then hugged—something unheard of on the streets of America, but very common in Italy—but when the man in the suit kissed the gondolier on the lips, I nearly dropped my bag in surprise.

Hugging, yes. Even kissing each other on each cheek, or—strange to Americans—patting each other on the behind, all of those things I'd seen. But a full kiss on the lips between two men? That could only mean one thing.

The encounter was over by the time I went outside, the man with the briefcase gone, but I couldn't help voicing my curiosity.

"Who was that?" I asked as Nico offered me a hand and I stepped onto the boat.

He glanced at me in surprise as I settled myself on a seat. "Just a friend."

"Looked like a *very* good friend," I remarked, hiding a knowing smile.

"He is, still." The gondolier untied and pushed off, and we were on our way again. "He lives in Sicily now. I see him very rarely. It was a coincidence to run into him here."

He was so cavalier about it, not embarrassed at all, but it was clear to me—Nico was gay. Which, I had to admit, relieved me of some of my trepidation, and I began to look back over our conversation with a different lens.

"So are you ready for a real Italian Shrove Tuesday?" he asked as we maneuvered back down the little canal. "My mother has been cooking all week for today. If we get there early enough, we can eat all the *Zeppole* before my sisters arrive. What do you say?"

I'd denied myself the revelry and masked silliness in the streets, but I had to admit, I'd been longing for some company, a little good food and wine and conversation. Who could turn down homemade Italian cooking on Carnavale? Why not?

Smiling, I accepted. "*Si, signor!* You've convinced me."

Nico smiled as we headed into the more open water of the Grand Canal, steering us toward his home.

"Nico brought a *girl* home!" Nico's mother—"Call me Mama Dorotea!"—stage-whispered into the phone to one of his sisters, glancing over at me perched on the edge of the sofa. I got the feeling Nico didn't bring girls home often—go figure—and they were all trying to be casual but I'd heard the phrase, "Nico brought a *girl* home!" at least ten times since I'd arrived.

"No, a *girl*." Mama Dorotea cupped the mouthpiece with her hand as she spoke, as if it might make sound travel slower in my direction. "Are you coming soon?"

That was the third daughter on the phone, I deduced—the other two were already present and accounted for. The oldest, Anna, was married and had two children, a boy and a girl, who ran straight to the kitchen when they arrived to "help" grandma with the food. Helping, of course, involved a great deal of tasting. The youngest daughter, Caprice, still a teenager, seemed intent on beating her older—and only—brother at Scrabble. Nico was sprawled out with her on the floor. Out of his gondolier uniform, wearing jeans and a gray pullover, he was even more handsome. It never failed—the cute ones were always gay.

"Another glass of wine, Daniella?"

"It's Dani," I corrected her again, accepting the glass from Anna, the oldest daughter. Her husband had parked himself in front of the television for a football game—which, in Italy, meant soccer—and hadn't said a word to anyone. His wife, on the other hand, had attached herself to me, talking almost non-stop since I arrived.

She paid no attention to my words, going on about the issues they were having with their flat, the landlord refusing to fix things. Nico, from the floor, offered to help repair the leaky sink, but Anna didn't listen to him either. She seemed more focused on complaining about her problems than she was on actually solving any of them.

I sipped my wine—homemade, according to Mama Dorotea—and watched Nico. Strangely, now that I knew he was gay, I gave myself more freedom to really look at him. His olive skin still retained a bit of a summer tan from working outside all year round. He was my age, probably early-to-mid-twenties, sandwiched somewhere between his younger teenage sister and the next oldest, who had just gotten married the year before. The siblings all had the same dark hair, the girls' long and thick and wavy, Nico's short and curly; the same striking, bright blue eyes; even the same full, sensual mouth.

Nico glanced up at me and winked, putting tiles down on the Scrabble board as his youngest sister protested using "Qi" as a word. I still couldn't believe I'd said I'd come to dinner, with his family no less. I was clearly more lonely that I wanted to admit. But he was sweet, and more importantly, he was safe. Maybe we could even be friends. I'd been in Italy eight months and didn't have any real friends to speak of, aside from Cara Lucia.

"I'm getting a dictionary!" Caprice jumped up, racing for the bookshelf in the corner.

"Look it up." Nico rolled to his back, putting his hands behind his head, and grinned. "Fifty-four points, triple letter, double word score. I win!"

"You're far too proud of yourself," I commented, sipping my wine to hide a smile. Beside me, Anna had thankfully been distracted by one of the children, the girl, Maria, coming in to ask her mother a question. Everyone spoke Italian and no one seemed to notice that I wasn't a native speaker. It was quite a compliment and I was rather proud of myself.

"You want to play the winner?" Nico asked me.

"You're so sure you're the winner."

"I am." He shrugged. "Qi is a word."

"It's not an Italian word," I replied. We were all speaking in Italian and I was proud of myself for holding my own. "I don't even think it's an English word."

"It's an Oriental word." Caprice sighed, reading from the dictionary. "Oriental medicine, martial arts, etcetera. The *vital energy believed to circulate around the body in currents.*"

"I win!" Nico pumped his fist in the air and his sister stuck her tongue out behind his back.

"Time to eat!" Mama Dorotea appeared in the doorway wearing an apron, stained and covered in flour. That was a good sign. My stomach was growling and I definitely needed to eat something—I'd had far too much wine on an empty stomach and my head was swimmy.

"What about Giulia and Will?" Anna herded her kids toward the dining room table.

"They're going to be late," Mama Dorotea announced, using the remote to turn off the television. It was the first time Anna's husband, Sal, had looked at something other than the screen since he sat down. He grunted, getting up, and followed his nose toward the table. "They said to start without them."

The family gathered around the food, practically drooling, as Mama Dorotea said a prayer, mentioning her dead husband at the end, asking the family to remember him. I'd noticed the urn and photo of the mustachioed man on the fireplace mantel when we came in and wondered how this woman had raised four children nearly to adulthood on her own.

"*Ti amo, Padre,*" Anna whispered at the end of the prayer, reaching over and squeezing her mother's hand. Mama Dorotea's eyes were shiny as she started passing around dishes full of gnocci, tortellini and castagnole. It didn't stay quiet for long. The two kids fought over who got the biggest and best piece of lasagna while Anna continued her diatribe about their dilapidated flat, and Caprice interjected with her own teen angst—a girl at school who liked the same boy who refused to speak to her now.

Nico sat next to me, passing me dish after dish, forcing me to fill my plate. There were frittelle— fritters fried to a perfect golden brown, filled with meat and gravy. The *migliaccio di polenta*—polenta and sausage—was so aromatic my stomach actually growled as I put some on my plate. I lost count after a while of how many plates were passed piled with all sorts of pastas filled with sweet prosciutto, smoky pancetta, and buttery sopressata.

"What did I tell you about the food?" Nico asked, nudging me, his mouth half-full. I could only whimper in response, sweet, heavenly pasta melting on my tongue. If there was something I loved almost as much as the Italian language, it was Italian food, and this was the best I'd ever had in nearly a year living in Italy.

"Nico made the lasagna," Mama Dorotea said, smiling over at me. "And the *Zeppole* for dessert. Wait until you taste!"

"You cook?" I managed, swallowing the perfect bite with a bit of wine.

His cheeks pinked up as he shoveled another mouthful in, not responding.

"Our Nico is the best cook in the family." Mama Dorotea reached over and ruffled his hair, making her son blush a deeper shade of red.

"Mama!" he protested, waving her away.

"It's true," Caprice piped up. "No one can outcook Nico."

"Nona Lara was better," Nico said, gulping his own wine. "My grandmother," he said to me. "She's who taught me how to cook."

"Nona Lara watched the children while I worked," Mama Dorotea explained. "She was here when they came home from school every day."

"We made dinner together every night," Nico said.

And now I had a clear picture of this family, the single, young widowed mother, a grandmother staying home to take care of the children while she worked. I hadn't been in the midst of any sort of family for a long time, and it felt good to be in the middle of the chatter, the teasing, the inside jokes I didn't understand but made me smile anyway. I didn't know if it was the wine, the food, or the people, but I was far more comfortable than I had expected to feel surrounded by strangers. It probably should have made me nostalgic for my own family, but my mother, although a single mother in her own right, had given me turkey TV-dinners on Thanksgiving and always confused my birthday with her own. It was hard to miss stuff like that.

"Thanks for inviting me," I whispered to Nico while the two kids argued with their mother about getting dessert if they hadn't finished their dinner. I saw his mother smile at us approvingly, saw the look she exchanged with her oldest daughter when Nico leaned in to say "You're welcome," into my ear.

"Mama!" A voice called from the other room and everyone looked up.

"They're here!" Mama Dorotea stood, putting her napkin down on the table and rushing toward the doorway. "They're here! They're here!"

"They're here!" The kids jumped up and followed and so did both Anna and Caprice. Only Sal sat unmoving, shoveling in huge mouthfuls of lasagna.

"You'd think the messiah had returned," I murmured, making Nico snort laughter beside me.

"You could say that," he replied with a smile. "You see, my sister and her husband—"

That was as far as he got before the whole lot of them burst into the room, all surrounding a pretty young woman with the same dark hair, hers cut shorter than the rest, curling around her cherubic face, her blue eyes bright with laughter.

"Let us take a breath!" the young woman—Giulia, I assumed—exclaimed, her gaze falling on her brother. "Can you help me, Nico?"

He stood, taking two strides toward his sister to take something from her arms. It took me a moment to register what it was, and by the time Nico had reached me, his sisters and mother following, exclaiming all around him, I felt rooted in my chair, trapped and speechless.

"Meet his highness, the Bianchi messiah, my sister's son, Luka—the first boy in the family since I was born." Nico pulled back the blue knitted blanket to show me the tiny face of a very newborn baby. He couldn't have been more than a week or two old, his little hand drawn up to his mouth, eyes screwed up tight as he sucked on his fingers.

Everyone was quiet now, focused on me and my reaction. I knew what I was supposed to do and say, but I couldn't find the words. They were caught in my throat.

"Give the woman a little room." It was Sal, Anna's husband, who spoke up. "You're overwhelming her."

And of course, he was absolutely correct.

"Excuse me." I managed to stand, grabbing the back of the chair for support, before bolting down the hall toward the bathroom. I sat on the commode, my head tucked between my knees, my whole body trembling. They were talking again, maybe about me, but it sounded more like they were exclaiming over the baby.

The baby.

Oh my God, I'd just run out of the room like an idiot. What must they think?

But I couldn't let them see me like this, shaking and holding back sobs and trying to draw breath into my lungs like a fish out of water. Sometimes the pain came out of nowhere and blindsided me. It was like getting hit upside the head by a two by four from behind. It just flattened me.

"Dani?" Nico knocked gently on the door, calling my name. I thought about not answering him, pretending I was invisible. That was ridiculous, of course. I was going to have to face him—face all of them.

"Just a moment," I called, hearing the quiver in my voice and cursing it. I stood, checking my face in the mirror—tear-streaked, nose red, mascara running. I was a mess.

"Come out," he called, knocking again. "Whatever it is, we don't have to talk about it."

How did he know just the right thing to say? I gravitated toward the door and unlocked it, peeking out. He must have seen my face, known I'd been crying. I hadn't washed it or tried to cover it up.

"I have something to show you." He extended his hand. "Come with me."

"I can't," I croaked, shrinking back. "You don't understand."

"Trust me."

"I hardly know you." I sniffed.

"Trust me anyway."

I took his offered hand and followed.

Chapter Two

Dear Carrie and Doc,

~~You're not going to believe~~

~~Remember how I said I wasn't interested in~~

Carnavale turned out to be a lot more interesting than I expected...

"Carnavale." He whispered the word into my ear. The city was laid out before us like brightly colored jewels on velvet. The lights of the parade and shows going on below in the Piazza lit up all of Venice. Each costumed dancer glittered like a piece of shiny candy we could have plucked up and eaten. I watched, enthralled, feeling Nico's warm breath against my cheek. Even in my desperate attempt to avoid the festivities, I couldn't help but be a part of them. Italy had a way of drawing you in, whether you liked it or not.

It was the most beautiful thing I'd ever seen.

"This is your place?" I asked, hugging myself as I looked down through the little window of the attic room.

"Yes." He peered over my shoulder and I felt him pressed against me, long and lean. "This way, I can have my own space, but also be near my family."

"You're close with them?"

He shrugged. "They're my family. I take care of them since my mother, she can't work anymore."

"She was a seamstress?" I remembered her talking about it.

"Her arthritis is too bad now for her to work."

"Thank you for showing me this." I turned slightly to look at him, his eyes gleaming silver in the darkness. "Thank you for inviting me today. About what happened... I'm sorry..."

"Come. Sit." He led me over to his bed and we perched on the edge, side by side. If I hadn't known he was gay, and if I hadn't had so much wine to drink, I wouldn't have followed him. I would have been on my guard and tense when he put his arm around me and held me close. But I felt safe with him, safer than I had with a single man in a long time, so I let him comfort me, settling in as we reclined on his bed, tucking my head under his chin.

"Do you want to talk about it, bella?"

Bella. He was just using a common Italian endearment, the word for beautiful. He couldn't have known the memories it triggered for me.

"No." I shook my head and held on, closing my eyes. "Can we just... not talk."

"Si." His lips brushed my forehead and I sighed in relief. If I'd had to explain, I would have broken down completely, shattered into a million little pieces that poor Nico would have had to pick up and somehow put back together before we went down to face his family.

Instead we held each other, the music of Carnavale playing below like the soundtrack of a distant dream. It was probably the wine coursing through me, making me far too warm in the chilly attic room. I hadn't had that much to drink in a long time, and even all the food we'd consumed hadn't dampened the buzzing in my head.

It was the wine—that's what I told myself when Nico began stroking my hair, sending little shivers through me. I reminded myself that this was impossible, that he was simply comforting a crazy woman he'd had the misfortune to invite into his home. That I was lucky he hadn't kicked me out at the first sign of insanity. And maybe we were both a little drunk and lonely and looking for comfort that night.

"Your family," I reminded him after a while, although I didn't want to move. I was sleepy and it felt so good to be held in a man's arms again, even if nothing was going to come of it. Maybe because nothing was going to come of it.

"Shhh." He kissed my forehead, tightening his arms around me. "Don't remind me."

I smiled. "We can't stay here forever."

"What happened to not talking?"

"But—"

I gasped in surprise when he silenced me with a kiss—and not a brotherly little kiss either, this was a full, hard sort of kiss that deepened the longer it went on. I felt faint when we broke apart, my limbs trembling.

"I'm sorry," he panted. "It was the best way I could think of to keep you quiet."

"It worked," I whispered, looking at him in the darkness, incredulous. This couldn't be happening. For all sorts of reasons.

He kissed me again, this time slower, exploring, his hand running down my side, over my hip, pulling my pelvis in against his. I moaned in response, shifting toward him, sliding my leg up over his.

I don't know how it happened. I told myself we were drunk, crazy with the sights of Carnavale. Like the masked revelers in the streets, we were anonymous, just heat and friction together in the darkness. I forgot about everything in his arms, giving in to pure sensation, letting instinct and desire alone guide me.

I think I tried to protest once, questioning his motives—and my own—but he drowned me with kisses, the weight of his body on mine a welcome relief from thought. His mouth slanted across mine and he wedged his thigh between my legs, rocking us on the bed to the faint beat of a distant drum. I clung to him, just as hungry as he was.

"Is this okay?" he gasped, kissing his way down my neck, opening the V of my blouse.

"Yes," I urged, daring to reach down and cup his crotch in response, sighing happily at the bulge found there. The heat of him through his jeans was incredible. I wrapped my legs around him, arching to give him better access as he fumbled with the front hook on my bra, the buttons of my blouse already undone to my waist. "Wait, did you lock the door?"

"Of course." His mouth moved over my breasts, leaving hot trails of saliva. I didn't even have time to register that he might have been planning this all along—or was it just an opportunity we both took? I still couldn't quite wrap my head around what I'd assumed—that he was definitely gay and not interested in me sexually—with what was happening now.

I thought about saying something, asking, clarifying—but I didn't want to break the mood.

It had been far too long since I'd let a man touch me, and with his hands and mouth roaming and the feel of his hard cock pressed against my hip, the word "no" seemed to have vanished from my vocabulary. Besides, Nico was not only attractive, he was clearly skilled. His tongue made hot circles around my nipple while he unzipped my jeans, sliding a hand inside to find the soft, hairless swell of my labia with his fingers.

"Smooth," he murmured, his eyes widening in surprise. I hadn't gone native, still keeping up with the American trend of shaving my pussy completely. "Oh bella, she's so soft..."

I squirmed as he began exploring, working my jeans down my hips, wanting to give him more. He helped me, tossing them aside as he settled himself between my thighs, my panties still on, the crotch already soaking wet. Nico brushed his cheek against the silk, breathing me in, and I ran a hand through his hair, my nails digging into his shoulders when his tongue found me through the material.

I hooked my thumbs in the elastic of my panties and peeled them down. Nico took them the rest of the way, splaying his big palms on my thighs and spreading me wider for his plunging tongue. I let him take what he wanted, my limbs quivering with an overload of sensation, my hips rocking in rhythm.

He paused only a moment to murmur, "You taste like heaven," diving back in again with stunning ability coupled with a ferocious enthusiasm that had me at the edge of orgasm in moments.

"Nico!" I gasped a warning, gripping his hair, my pelvis undulating, belly quaking, poised at the brink. His fingers sent me over, dipping deep into my pussy, drawing me out, his tongue punishing my clit with sensation, drowning me with pleasure. I tried to be quiet, too mindful of where we were, who might come knocking on the door, but I couldn't help crying out with my climax, my body quaking as if the earth had moved beneath me.

"Beautiful," he whispered, kissing his way up my quivering belly, cupping his whole hand over my mound as we kissed, making me whimper and melt against him. He was fully clothed still, his belt buckle nibbling at my hip, and I moved to rectify that situation, pulling his shirt off, exploring muscle and sinew and flesh in the dark.

He was just as eager as I was, helping me with his belt and zipper, shoving his jeans down his hips. His cock sprang free when I pulled his boxers down, first into my hand and then into my greedy mouth. Nico reclined on the bed, letting me suck him. It had been so long since I'd had a cock in my mouth, since I'd tasted the peppery promise of cum accumulating in clear, sticky droplets at the tip. I was dizzy with desire.

"Here." He guided me, a fist in my hair, nice and easy, up and down his delicious length. I tasted him in my throat, an easy burn, the promise of more roiling in the tightening scrotum I held cupped in my palm. "Oh God. Yes. Oh yes, bella, yes!"

I wanted to taste him, to feel the flood of his cum over my tongue, but Nico had other ideas. He stopped me, easing his cock out of my mouth and rubbing it over my lips and cheeks and tongue. Then he reached for me, pulling me into the circle of his arms and rolling me onto my back on the mattress, kissing me quiet.

His cock was heated steel between my legs, riding the rails, dipping into the valley of my pussy. The tip teased my sensitive clit, everything slippery wet, before sliding down and finding my entrance. He did this without looking, just feeling his way, hips shifting forward when he felt my flesh give, sliding into me.

"Oh my fucking God." I said the words in English, surprising us both.

"Good?" He propped himself up on his arms to look down at me in the darkness, the only light coming from the window, a silvery haze.

"Si!" I assured him in Italian, sliding my hands up the muscled flesh of his arms, delighting in the mountains and valleys of his shoulders. "It's been so long... so very long..."

"For me too." He bent his head to my neck, beginning to move inside of me, his swollen length creating a delicious friction. "I might not last so long..."

"It's okay," I assured him, although part of me never wanted it to end. He felt far too good.

"I'll try..." He panted in my ear. "Ahhhh God you're so wet..."

I was. I slid my hand down to touch him, feeling his length where he went into me, the place where we were joined. My pussy was on fire, my clit aching for more, and I touched myself as he fucked me, closing my eyes with pleasure.

"Good girl," he encouraged, forcing my thighs open further with his, changing the angle of penetration, making us both moan. "Oh fuck."

"Yes!" I cried, rubbing faster, faster. "Oh please, yes, fuck me, Nico! Fuck me hard!"

He gave into it, not holding back anymore, and the force of him left me breathless, driving me into the soft press of his mattress again and again. I watched him in the faint light from the window, seeing his face change, his eyes squeezing closed, his lower lip drawn between his teeth. His cock was like granite, the heat between our legs a river of lava.

"Come for me," I begged, squeezing him hard with the muscles of my pussy, his eyes flying open in surprise. "Oh God, yes, yes, Nico, come with me, come with me!"

My climax swallowed me up in one quivering mass, spitting me back out into reality, shivering and dizzy and gasping for air. I hung onto him as he came too, hiding the sound of my name in the soft, moist crook of my neck as he shuddered into me, the hot flood of his cum pulsing through us both.

It took me a long time to recover. He rolled to the side, pulling a sheet over us, and we breathed together in the darkness. At first I couldn't focus, but when rational thought finally returned, I remembered where I was, who I was with, what we'd done. It wouldn't be the first time in my life I'd had sex with a stranger, but it was the first time in a very long time.

"Well, I think this was indulgent enough for Fat Tuesday," I murmured, feeling Nico stir beside me.

He chuckled. "We don't call it 'Fat Tuesday' in Italy. Here, it's Shrove Tuesday. Do you know what that means?"

I'd heard the term but had no idea what it meant. "No."

"It means to confess. Have you ever been to confession?"

I smiled. "No."

"It's very freeing, to be absolved of all of your sins," he assured me, tracing my navel with his finger. "Today we confess, and for Lent, we do penance."

"You deny yourself?" I asked. "What will you give up?"

"We have to give up something we really love for it to be true penance," he explained. "I considered giving up sex, but now... perhaps I'll give up chocolate instead."

"Good call." I laughed.

"So what do you have to confess?" he asked, leaning over and kissing the side of my breast, his fingers tracing light patterns over my skin.

"Far too much for the time we have." I slid my arm around his neck and kissed his cheek, grateful when a knock came on the door.

"Nico!" It was Mama Dorotea and the sound of her voice had us both scrambling for our clothes. "Why is the door locked? What are you doing? Your sister is leaving, you should come say goodbye!"

We fumbled with buttons and zippers, Nico making excuses the whole while, assuring his mother we'd be right down. Thankfully Giulia and Will and the baby were already gone and I didn't have to make any explanations. When Nico offered to take me home, I refused, telling him I preferred to walk. I needed to clear my head, I said. That much was true.

But it was only about ten blocks, and I would have needed a far greater distance to accomplish that goal, I realized, as I approached the front steps of Cara Lucia's. I saw the light on in her window up front, heard laughter inside. I felt as if I'd been part of a family again tonight for the first time in so long. I hadn't felt a part of things that way since Carrie and Doc had practically adopted me, and it had woken something in me I had almost forgotten about.

"There you are!" Cara Lucia opened her door as I made my way down the hall. How she'd known I was there was beyond me. The woman seemed to have extrasensory perception. She stood only five-foot-two and her graying hair was pulled up and back, her aging face still quite beautiful. Her daughters looked just like her—all five of them. I could hear them laughing and talking inside. "Come to celebrate Carnavale?"

I felt guilty about not accepting her earlier invitation. I didn't see any of her other boarders—most of them foreign exchange students—sitting at the dining room table. Had she invited them as well? Or just me, I wondered? I'd had lunch with her almost every week at that table, talking about her husband and daughters, my studies, my life—before. She was probably the closest thing I had to a friend in Italy.

But I still shook my head, smiling. "No, I'm sorry, I've had enough celebrating today, I think."

"I have something for you, wait." She held up one finger, leaving the door open a crack.

"No, that's—"

She had disappeared already, so I waited, sure she was bringing me a care package, more food to add to the calorie-laden meal I'd eaten today. I smiled, remembering Nico's family. Remembering Nico. Just thinking about him made my head swim. What had I gotten myself into?

Cara Lucia reappeared, something small in her palm. Definitely not the care package I'd expected. She held it out, smiling, gesturing for me to take it. "For you."

The necklace was beautiful, a gold ellipse with a green stone set in the center. "Oh, no, I can't possibly accept this."

"It is the emerald eye of Beatrice." She was already folding it into my hand. "I thought of you and your work with Dante Alighieri and knew you must have it."

She knew that I was doing my thesis on *The Inferno.*

"That is so sweet of you." Of course, now I felt doubly guilty for not taking her up on attending her Carnavale celebration. "Thank you, Cara Lucia." I leaned over to kiss her cheek.

She beamed. "Perhaps your Dante will return to his Beatrice."

"You mean Mason?" I blinked, looking down at the charm in my hand. It had never occurred to me that my ex-husband might be my Dante—the doomed love of my life, a relationship destined to end in tragedy, at least on the worldly plane of existence.

"He redeemed himself in the end, you know," Cara Lucia reminded me with a wink.

"And Beatrice might have been better off if she'd just let him go," I countered, turning the charm over in my hand. I had to admit, I was thinking of Nico.

When I looked up at Cara Lucia, I saw the speculative look in her eyes. I'd told her a great deal—probably too much—about my relationship with my ex and everything that had happened when it all fell apart. "Anyway, thank you. It's beautiful."

"L'esperîenza di questa dolce vita," she murmured, squeezing my hand. It was a quote from Dante—*the experience of this sweet life.* "It is yours, Cara," she told me, using the endearment her own man had given her years ago. Cara meant 'beloved' and she had been called Cara Lucia her whole life because her husband couldn't speak her name without putting his love for her first. "It is all of ours."

I thanked her again for the charm, promising to come by next week some time for lunch, going upstairs and down the hallway to my own room. Jezebel was waiting, mewing impatiently for her own Carnavale feast. So we sat on my little bed and listened to Venice celebrating and I hand-fed her the bread and cheese I had been expecting to eat for my own dinner.

So many things had happened that I hadn't been expecting today. What else did the experience of this life have in store? I wondered, looking at the charm. So far, aside from a few bright moments, life hadn't been very sweet to me. But maybe I was just being ungrateful. I put the necklace on and found myself thinking of Nico with a little spark of hope.

I had come to Italy for so many things, including the great food, of course, but sometimes I just wanted a good old American cheeseburger. The Mood Café had the best cheeseburgers around, and that's where I told Nico I'd meet him for lunch. He was late, and I was already eating, drinking a vanilla Coke and dipping my fries in hot mustard, when I saw him walking up the cobblestone street.

The day was bright, a little chilly, but I'd decided to sit outside anyway. Italians were oblivious to the weather. In America, life was about comfort. In Italy, it was about experience. If it was cold, you were cold. If it was hot, you were hot. If it was raining, they didn't care. In the summer, there was no air conditioning anywhere, and it was hot as hell—but no one cared. Those weren't problems to be fixed, but rather things to be experienced.

I smiled as he approached, seeing his eyes light up when he saw me. I couldn't help my body's instant response when he bent to kiss my cheek, remembering his lips, his mouth, his hands. It still felt like a dream, like something that had happened to someone else and not to me.

"Thank you for waiting, bella," he murmured against my ear.

"Last minute gondola customer?" I guessed, smiling at the waiter as he refilled my water glass and took Nico's order—cheeseburger, fries and cherry Coke.

"My mother." He sipped his own glass of water. "She asked me to come home to help her move a table."

I blinked. "And you left work for that?"

"I didn't have any customers." He shrugged. "Carnavale is over and the tourists have all gone home."

"But you had a lunch date with me," I reminded him.

"And here I am." He spread his hands, *taa-daa*, and smiled.

"Yes, here you are." *Late,* I thought, but didn't say it. "So tell me something..."

"Anything." He reached over and snagged one of my fries, crunching happily and grinning at me. There was something about him that made me want to smack him and kiss him at the same time. He reminded me of someone, but I couldn't quite put my finger on who.

"How do you become a gondolier exactly?"

"Do you have career ambitions?" He raised an eyebrow and then laughed. "The training is actually quite extensive. You have to go through a year-long apprenticeship and take several tests."

"Really?" I moved my plate out of his reach when he went for another fry. "I had no idea it was so involved."

"The association actually caps the number of gondoliers they'll allow to work in the city." His gaze wandered to the people passing on the street and I noticed a pretty blonde—and noticed him noticing her.

"So it's kind of an exclusive club." I offered him a fry, a distraction. I didn't blame him for looking—the woman was stunning—but I also didn't feel like competing.

"I suppose it is." He took my peace offering. "My father was a gondolier and my father before him."

"Wow. So it's a legacy. Sounds like you were destined to do it."

"You'd think so, wouldn't you?" He smiled thinly as the waiter appeared with his cheeseburger. Nico dug in immediately, wolfish, talking with his mouth half full. "So what are you going to do with your degree?"

"Probably find a job in the states doing translation. Spending lots of time traveling back to Italy for business." I watched him swallow a huge bite of cheeseburger, washed down with a swig of cherry Coke. "At least, I hope."

He paused, chewing his last bite thoughtfully before swallowing. "Why don't you stay here, work here... live here?"

"I've thought about it," I admitted, seeing the hopeful look on his face and deciding to change the subject. "I have to tell you something."

"Oh?"

The blonde was coming back this way and I saw his gaze shift again as she passed.

"I'm embarrassed to admit it."

He smiled, looking back at me. "Confession is good for the soul, remember?"

"Okay... the truth is..." I cleared my throat, glancing first at the disappearing shape of the blonde and then over to the waiter, as if someone might overhear. "Before yesterday, I was under the impression that you were gay."

He laughed. "Why would you think so?"

"When you dropped me off at the post office, you were talking to a man," I explained. "Well, not just talking..."

"Ohhh!" His eyes brightened with understanding. "Well, then I guess I have a confession to make as well."

"You really are gay and I was just a fling?"

"No." He smiled. "I'm bisexual."

Well that explained everything, didn't it?

"Does that bother you?" he asked.

"Actually, no." I sat back in my chair, making yet another confession. "So am I."

He looked surprised. "You have been with both men and women?"

I nodded. "My last committed relationship was with both a man and a woman."

"Interesting." He went back to working on his cheeseburger, already halfway through, chewing thoughtfully. "I've been with men—and women—but never both together."

"You should." I grinned. "I highly recommend it."

"So how did this happen?"

I considered not telling him—I'd kept my relationship with the Baumgartners a secret, not something I was ashamed of, but more like something precious that might be spoiled by sharing it—but he looked so curious and interested and open that I confessed that too.

"I met Carrie and Doc about a year before I left for Italy."

"Tell me about them."

And so I did. I told him about meeting Carrie and Doc, about their slow seduction and my ending up in love with them both. It had been an amazing year of my life, something I'd fallen into while my marriage to Mason fell apart. They weren't the cause of the end of my relationship with my ex, but they were both there to pick up the messy pieces, and I would always be grateful to them for that.

"Both of them? You loved them both?" Nico cocked his head at me.

I nodded. "I did. I do."

"But they are married?"

"Yes, and very much committed to each other," I explained. "They loved me and included me, but it was always clear that theirs was the primary relationship. And I was okay with that."

"Fascinating."

Of course, I left out the part about being in the middle of a messy divorce from Mason at the time. That didn't seem relevant. Or maybe I was just kidding myself.

"You are a mystery, bella." He was done with his meal, leaving a few fries on his plate, an afterthought, and he leaned over to take my hand.

"Nico..." I looked down our hands twined together on the table, remembering the way our bodies melded, dissolved, becoming one. "I can't help feeling like we've opened Pandora's Box."

"Yes, perhaps we have," he agreed, rubbing his thumb against the crease in my palm. "But the thing is, you can't close it once it's been opened."

"Do you want to?"

"Me?" He grinned. "Hell no."

We both sat back as the waiter appeared, refilling water glasses and asking if we needed anything. We dismissed him as quickly as we could, wanting to keep our focus on each other. I could feel the energy between us, hotter than any sun, and I couldn't help but turn my face toward it.

"Do you have to go back to class this afternoon?" Nico inquired, leaning in again.

"No." I met his eyes, full of wanting. "Do you have to go back to work?"

"I should." He shrugged. "But I don't want to."

I bit my lip, tracing the wet rim of my water glass. "What if I asked you to come back to my room?"

Nico half stood, waving at the waiter. "Check!"

⌑ ⌑ ⌑

"Shhh!" I begged him to be quiet. Cara Lucia was home and while she was, thankfully, hard of hearing, she wasn't completely deaf. I'd had to sneak him in, up the back stairway, which happened to be right next to my room. Lucky me. The other students weren't so fortunate—two of them had been caught already this year sneaking paramours into their rooms and one had actually been asked to leave. He couldn't seem to stop inviting women to his room. I definitely didn't want to be kicked out—real estate was at a premium and rooms were hard to find for students.

"Sorry," he apologized, catching me in his arms as I shut the door. "I can't keep my hands off you."

"Do you want some coffee?" I headed for my little kitchenette, petting Jezebel on the way. She had come out to investigate the intruder, sniffing at Nico's pant leg as he followed me. Cara Lucia's rooms were designed for exchange students. We had our own bath and shower in each, but just a kitchenette—no stove but a small refrigerator, hot plate, a little table and two chairs.

"I have tea. Some juice?"

"I don't want anything but you." Nico sat on one of the chairs, scratching Jezebel behind the ears. "Come here."

I did and he slid his hands around my waist and pulled me close, nuzzling my belly as Jezebel twined around our legs.

Nico sighed dreamily. "I think I'm addicted to you."

I relented, following the slope of his shoulders, feeling the muscles there, as he looked up at me, smiling. "So your mother and sisters seemed surprised you brought a woman home."

He shrugged. "I don't do it often."

"Why me?"

"I don't know." He shook his head, his eyes bright with humor. "Are you a witch?"

"Sometimes." I grinned. "And here I thought I'd converted you."

"No." He chuckled. "But a woman like you could definitely convert a gay man."

"You like what you see?"

His gaze moved over my breasts, outlined by the tight fit of my sweater. "Very much."

"It's different in the day time." We had seen so little of each other in his room. The experience had been just flesh and heat and sensation.

"Yes," he agreed.

He kissed me, his mouth soft and open, drawing me in. I let him explore with his tongue, let his hands roam over the soft material of my sweater, even let him rub the seam of my jeans between my legs.

"You're so beautiful," he said, lifting my sweater to feather kisses around my navel. I pulled my sweater off over my head, revealing a pale, pink bra underneath. He smiled and teased my dark nipples through the sheer material, making them harden. I bit my lip as he slid his hands up to my waist and pulled me closer, his tongue lapping at my nipples through my bra, making wet spots.

"I want to see all of you."

I let him undress me, my jeans joining my sweater on the floor. The panties matched the bra—I had put them on with the forethought that he might end up seeing them today—and he licked along the top edge of the elastic, making me shiver with anticipation.

"Let's go to bed," I suggested, taking his hand and leading him. He was still fully dressed, but I wasn't having any more of that. I sat on the edge of my bed and he let me undress him, unbuttoning his shirt, opening it to reveal the hard planes of his chest, the ridges of his belly. His jeans were next, his cock already nicely tenting his boxers. I knew the feel of it already, but the sight of it was spectacular, the way it curved up toward my mouth when I freed him so inviting I had to take his length between my lips.

"Oh yes," he whispered, hands in my hair, urging me on. The thick, black nest of his pubic hair tickled my nose as took all of him into my mouth, watching his face change as I began to really suck him. "Oh that's so good!"

His praise just made me work harder, taking him in my fist too, using both hand and mouth to pleasure him. He began to thrust his hips, easing his swollen length in and out between my lips, reaching down to cup my breast while I sucked him. It was easy to become eager, greedy. It had been so long for me, and having a cock in my mouth made me melt into a puddle of lust.

"Easy," he urged, sliding his cock out of my mouth, rubbing it over my lips, my waiting tongue. "So hungry."

"You have no idea."

He smiled, pushing me back on the bed, the weight of him delightful as he kissed me. I wrapped my arms around his neck, feeling the hard press of his thigh between mine, the wet, shaved lips of my pussy like a hot suction cup against his leg. He groaned softly against my mouth as I began to ride him like that, using the length of his thigh to rub myself off.

His mouth moved down to my breasts, teasing one nipple and then the other, sending shockwaves through my body. I looked down at his dark, curly head in wonder—how had this happened? His hand was wrapped around the length of his cock, not stroking, just squeezing, the mushroom tip red and swollen. It made my mouth water and my pussy clench.

"I want to taste you."

I didn't object. He kissed his way down my belly, my breath held, making it concave. Parting my lips with one finger, he began to explore the soft, pink folds of flesh like a maze or a roadmap. I felt his breath on my thighs and spread them wider for him in encouragement. He smiled, kissing the top of my cleft, so near my clit but not quite touching it, making me whimper with anticipation.

"Beautiful," was the last thing he said before covering my pussy with his mouth.

His tongue flicked gently at my clit, back and forth at first, then in easy circles. I lifted my hips when his fingers found the entrance of my pussy, probing, easing their way in. My flesh swallowed his fingers, eager for more, and he pumped them in and out as he licked me, driving me higher and higher.

"Oh yes!" I cried when he slid in a third, stretching me wide, his mouth fastened over my mound. "Fuck me like that! Harder!"

I heard him moan against my pussy, his fingers moving into me, deep and hard, the motion shaking my whole pelvis, making the bedsprings squeak and my hips rock up to meet his hand. I couldn't help it. It felt so good I could hardly keep from screaming—and I'd been the one telling him to be quiet!

"Yes, yes, yes!" I twisted my hips, feeling his fingers turning inside of me, his tongue tracing delicious geometry all over the sensitive bud of my clit. "Oh fuck! You're gonna make me come all over your face!"

And that's just what I did, spreading my legs and thrusting up to meet his flickering tongue, his pounding fingers, my orgasm tearing through me like a whirlwind, leaving me shaking in its wake. I was still recovering when he kissed me, letting me taste the musky milk of my pussy on his tongue.

"Tastes good, no?"

I nodded, licking at his lips and chin, making my way down his chest, rolling him to his back. His nipples were hard and I flicked them with my tongue, making him shiver in response, his eyes half-closed, watching my descent.

"Your turn," I teased, tracing circles around his navel with my fingernail, following the dark treasure trail leading down from belly button to pubic hair. His cock was wet with pre-cum.

"Don't make me come," he warned before I'd even taken him into my mouth. "I want your pussy."

"And she wants you," I purred, skipping his cock altogether and heading straight for his balls. They were heavy in my hands and I rolled them gently, grazing them with my fingernails. He moaned encouragement when I began to lick them, teasing his sac, watching pre-cum seep from the head of his cock in sticky, clear rivulets.

"Oh God!" He moaned when my fingers found their way down between the crack of his ass, pressing gently, teasing that dimpled recess. "Oh yes!"

Encouraged, I left my finger there when I took him into my mouth, watching his face twist with pleasure when I inserted it up to the first knuckle. I'd had plenty of men do this to me—but very few who would let me do it to them. It was a delightful, and very exciting, surprise.

"You need to stop," he murmured as I began to pump my finger in and out, the same rhythm I was using with my mouth on his cock. "Before I come in your mouth."

"I don't mind," I gasped, taking him out of my mouth only long enough to say the words.

"I do." He pulled me off again, biting his lip as I slowly slid my finger out of his ass. "Come here."

He settled me on top of him, his cock rising toward my navel, making an exclamation point between us. His hands roamed easily over my body, belly, breasts, hips, thighs, as if he could discover my flesh like a blind man reads Braille. I reached down to press the wet head of his cock against my belly, rubbing it gently in circles with my palm, seeing his eyes half-close at the sensation.

"I want to be inside of you."

He didn't need to ask me twice.

I went up to my knees, squeezing his cock as I aimed it, his gaze focused between my legs as I slid down his length. He parted my wet flesh easily, his hands moving to my hips, guiding me, in control, even with me on top of him. I slid my palms along his chest, letting the dark hair there curl around my fingers, teasing his nipples, grazing them lightly with my fingernails.

"You're naughty," he murmured as I rocked, a nice, slow ride. My nipples were so hard they ached, and he thumbed them, making me moan in response.

"Here," I said, guiding his hand down to my pussy, whimpering when his fingers found my clit. "Yes. Oh God yes, like that."

I felt his cock swell inside of me as I began to rock faster, matching his rhythm against my clit. Our breath came faster, our bodies starting to sheen with sweat. Sex in the light of day gave us both a new perspective, and I found myself looking into his eyes as we fucked, seeing far too much emotion there and wondering if he saw the same in mine.

"Fuck me from behind," I said, loathe to take him out of me, but not knowing if I could stand seeing the hungry look in his eyes anymore.

"Like a dog?" He chuckled as I got to my hands and knees on the bed, offering my ass up for the taking.

"Yes." I closed my eyes, feeling his hands on my hips, his cock already seeking entrance. "Fuck me like a dog."

I meant it, and I think he knew it. He shoved deep into me, the angle tighter now, better for us both. I reached under and rubbed my clit as he fucked me, the sound of us filling the room, two animals in heat, rutting together.

"Harder!" I hissed. "Deeper!"

He thrust again, again, grunting with the effort, giving me what I wanted, and I loved him for it. I was going to come like this with his cock buried so deep I could almost taste it, my pussy stretched with the glorious width of him.

"So tight," he moaned, lost too, and I found him with my hand, feeling him driving into me, using the heel of my palm to rub myself off. "Oh God, I can't... I can't..."

"Come on!" I urged, lifting my ass higher to meet him. "Do it! Oh fuck! Fuck!"

And then we were coming together, quivering and trying to drown our cries so no one heard the sounds of our lust. My eager pussy convulsed around the pulsing length of his cock, milking him, draining him completely. Nico collapsed onto me, the hard, lean, sweaty length of his body so good against mine I thought I must be dreaming this, all of this.

I even asked him, "Am I dreaming?" as he rolled to the side and gathered me into his arms.

"If you are, then I'm dreaming too."

I considered the possibility, touching the charm around my neck as we drifted in the hazy afternoon sunshine, wondering which would be better—dream or reality.

Chapter Three

Dear Carrie and Doc,

Janie sounds like a handful! The pictures you sent of her in the outfit Cara Lucia made were so sweet it made my uterus skip a beat. She's growing so fast!

Remember that guy I told you about, the gondolier, Nico? We've been seeing more of each other. A lot more of each other. I'm not ready to call it a relationship yet, although his mother and sisters have us practically married with two kids in their heads already. Mama Dorotea talks about wedding dress fabric every time I see her and shushes Nico when he insists her arthritis is too far gone for her to be sewing. Never mind that she's talking about sewing a wedding dress for a nonexistent wedding!

But in spite of all the mama's boy stuff—why do I pick men who can't cut the apron strings?—can I just say, in all honestly, I haven't had sex like this in so long. He reminds me a little of you, Doc—so insatiable. And Carrie, you'd like him. Oh what fun we could have with Nico, you and I! That is, if Doc didn't get too jealous. I know how he gets about sharing you, even if you're okay with things the other way around. The more I watch people and the relationships around me, the more I realize how special you two really are. You're in your own category altogether as far as I'm concerned. I don't think many people get to experience what we did together. And yes, I miss it, and I miss you.

Maybe it's because I deprived myself for so long, I don't know, but I can't get enough of Nico. And he... oh my God, he is a greedy boy. My little room at Cara Lucia's has paper-thin walls and while we can sneak up to his attic room at his mother's, I feel funny about it, and it's clear she doesn't approve. So we find ourselves looking for alternatives and I'm beginning to think we need to get our own place just so we don't get arrested!

"Not here," I whispered as Nico kissed me into a narrow alleyway, the cool brick biting my back, pressed hard against the wall.

"Yes here," he insisted, and I cursed myself for wearing a skirt to school. March was flirting with April and the weather had been sunny and bordering on warm all day, prompting my choice of outfit.

"No, no," I protested, but telling him no was impossible. He took what he wanted, when he wanted. I couldn't deny him, and even as my mind forbid him, my body responded, my hips thrusting to meet the hard press of his cock through his trousers, my mouth opening under his.

"I can't wait," he murmured, his hand cupping my mound through my skirt. "I've been thinking about you all day. My cock has been hard for hours."

"We could get caught," I whispered, eyes closed with pleasure as he rocked the heel of his palm against my pussy. It was still daylight and anyone passing by the alleyway could see us. "Arrested. What would your mother say?"

"I don't care," he growled, yanking my skirt up to my waist, exposing the black flash of my panties underneath.

"Nico!" I gasped when he went to his knees, unmindful of the suit he was wearing, burying his face between my legs.

The truth was, I was already soaking wet—I'd been thinking about him all day too, about our date and where we would go to ease this ache. I had to sneak him into my flat past Cara Lucia. His mother guarded his place like Fort Knox. We had found places of course, the darkness our accomplice. We had christened the restroom at the Mood Café twice, once in the men's room, the second time in the women's. We'd made love in the gondola in the dark several times, tied to a post, nearly tipping it over once in a narrow canal with our fervor. We'd even done it like this, in dark alleys, cul-de-sacs, entryways to empty buildings.

But we'd never dared to do it like this, in the daylight, in plain sight. I usually felt like a naughty teenager, sneaking around and hiding our lust, but this was beyond daring—it was dangerous.

I loved it.

"Lick it," I begged, sliding my leg up over his shoulder to give him better access. He nudged my panties aside and did just as he was told, his mouth working sweet, hot magic between my legs. My clit throbbed against his tongue, my nipples hardening under my blouse. I rubbed my own breasts, grazing them with my nails through the material, sending hot tingles down between my thighs.

"Oh God!" I cried when he grabbed my other thigh, pulling both of my legs over his shoulders. I looked down and could only see his curly head and the lust in those striking blue eyes on mine, his mouth fastened over my pussy. "Oh my God! Nico! Oh! Oh!"

I was coming, just like that, flooding his mouth, my clit beating time, like a hummingbird's wings, against the lash of his tongue. He moaned softly, his fingers digging into my ass, when he felt the buck of my hips, the arch of my back.

"I have to have you," he croaked, his face shiny with the juices from my pussy as he looked up at me, still on his knees, his eyes filled with something—a cross between desire and worship—that made me grateful he was still supporting me, because my knees suddenly felt weak.

When he shifted and stood, pressing me against the wall, I glanced down the alleyway, mindful now that we might be seen. I saw someone walk past, close enough I could tell it was a man pushing a cart, but he didn't glance toward us. The other way was a dead end, but there were doorways all along the alley, backs of shops, and owners or employees could come out of any one of those doors.

"Nico, wait," I murmured, feeling him fumble for his zipper, but once his cock was free, I truly couldn't resist. The hard length of him pressing against my thigh as he kissed me was pure temptation and I found him with my hand, feeling him swell as I began to stroke him. He moved his hips, seeking entrance, but I had other ideas.

"Ohhh *Mio Dio!*" he moaned as I sank to my knees for him, the cobblestone cold and unforgiving, but I didn't care. I sucked the thick, mushroom head of his cock, feeling his hand moving through my hair, pushing himself further into my throat. I let him thrust deep and hard, let him use my mouth for his pleasure, my fingernails grazing his balls, coaxing the cum I knew was boiling there to the surface.

"No, no, no," he cried, making a fist in my hair and pulling me back. I looked up at him, panting with lust, my eyes half-closed, my hand tucked between my legs, rubbing at my aching clit.

"Please," I whispered.

That was all I had to say. He stood, turning me around roughly and shoving me up against the wall. His hands roamed over my ass as he pulled my hips back, bending me at the waist so he could take me from behind. I braced myself, hands splayed on the brick, waiting for him to impale me.

"Play with yourself," he ordered, pulling me back into the saddle of his hips, his cock an iron rod between my ass cheeks.

"Please," I said again, but I reached down to touch myself, my clit pulsing under my fingers.

I heard a noise behind us and turned my head to look but Nico grabbed my hair, pressing my cheek to the wall as his cock slid into the wet, waiting shelter of my pussy. I prayed it was just a cat, but then he was fucking me and I forgot everything.

He grabbed onto my breasts, rubbing them through the silky material of my blouse, his cock a driving piston between my thighs. Already in heels, I went up on my toes, wanting all of him, deeper, harder. He fucked me so hard it hurt, and still I wanted more, the motion jarring, shoving me against the brick, rattling my pelvis, my breasts swaying in his hands.

"Don't stop," I begged, hearing the panting of his breath in my ear, feeling sweat trickling down the middle of my back underneath my bra strap, knowing he must be close. "Make me come! Oh fuck, Nico, please make me come again!"

He grabbed my thigh and lifted it, spreading me wide and pushing himself deeper inside of me, making me howl like an alley cat in heat. My fingers worked furiously against my clit, rubbing faster than Aladdin looking for that elusive genie, the anticipation of the wish almost better than its fulfillment.

Almost.

"I'm gonna come!" I cried, my body stretched taut, something in my belly poised and ready to spring. "Oh now! Now, now, now!

My pussy clamped down on his cock, spasming around his swollen length, a wet, velvet trap. He cried out at the sensation, grabbing my breasts and squeezing hard, his hips driving in deep, thrusting uncontrollably.

"Oh *mio Cara, mio amore,*" he whispered endearments into my ear, wrapping his arms around my waist and burying his face into my neck.

Self-conscious now, I pulled my skirt down, the slick slide of his cum caught only by the panties now bunched between my thighs. Nico zipped his pants, still breathing hard, and turned me to face him, kissing me deeply. I could taste myself on his tongue.

"You're a naughty girl."

"Me?" I gave a throaty laugh. "This alley was your idea."

"I can't resist you, bella." He kissed my lips, my cheek, my chin. "I've never met a woman who makes me want her like you do."

Beside us, a door opened, and a tall man stepped out carrying a bag of garbage. He took one look at us and rolled his eyes.

"Rent a room!" he growled, striding past us.

I looked at Nico and giggled. "You know we're going to be late for dinner at *Il Ridotto*!"

"No we're not. Come on."

"I can't run in these heels!" I protested as he dragged me along.

"Do you want me to carry you?"

I squealed when he bent and then hefted me up over his shoulders in a fireman's carry, my hair flying behind me. It was only a few blocks, but he ran the whole way with me on his shoulders, howling all the while.

"Shhh, you little she-wolf." He set me down and kissed me, barely out of breath. The man was in incredible shape. I smoothed my hair and my skirt, still flushed from being carried upside down—and from the sex. "Let's go eat. I'm starving."

Il Ridotto was so small it could only accommodate four couples and two more groups of four. The tables lined one wall with candles and a single flower in a vase in the center. The walls were light brick, the fixtures nondescript. People didn't come for the décor and the atmosphere—they came for the food and the wine.

A rotund man in an apron and a chef's hat came around the corner as the door closed, waving us in. There were two couples seated already, one of them eating, the other talking over glasses of wine.

"We have reservations," I explained as the little chef came our way. "Bianchi."

"Come in, come in!" He was boisterous and smiling, nodding his head as he showed us to our table. "I'm Gianni Bonaccorsi, I'll be your waiter—and your chef."

Nico had prepared me for this fact. Dinner at *Il Ridotto* was an intimate affair. Gianni handed over our menus and a wine list, excusing himself to let us look over the fare.

"Are you sure you can afford this?" I whispered behind my menu to Nico. As a student, I didn't make any money. I was living off savings and had to be very careful with it.

"Shush." He waved my question away. "Anything for you."

And that didn't exactly make me feel better about looking over the menu, where the items were fresh, local, gourmet, and very expensive.

"I can't possibly decide," I said, looking helplessly at Nico. "It all sounds so good!"

"I can order for us," he offered, and so when Gianni returned, I let him do just that, sitting back and enjoying the exchange between the two men.

Both of them clearly loved food and talking about it. Gianni spent fifteen minutes telling us about changes on the menu, letting us know what he got fresh at the market just that morning. When they got into discussing wine, I excused myself to go to the bathroom. I knew I had to be a mess—there was only so much I could do without a mirror.

I surveyed the damage as best I could in the little mirror over the sink, adjusting my dress at the top where my bra strap was still showing, touching up my makeup, running a comb through my hair. Satisfied that it was good enough, in spite of the flush still in my cheeks, I returned to the table to find Gianni and Nico sharing a complimentary glass of port from a fifteen-year-old bottle, laughing about something as if they were old friends.

"Salute!" Gianni offered me a glass, smiling as he raised his own and gave a popular Italian toast. *"Possa tu vivere cento anni!"*

"Salute!" Nico agreed, and we clinked glasses. The port was smooth and reminded me of cherries.

"I'm not sure I want to live a hundred years though," I commented as Gianni went off to get our antipasti.

"And why not?" Nico raised an eyebrow. "Isn't life good to you, bella?"

"Sometimes yes." I shrugged one shoulder, glancing over at one of the other couples. They were older, in their fifties, but they still smiled at each other and touched hands, offering each other bites of their food. It was a lovely sight and made my heart hurt. "Sometimes no."

"So tell me." He leaned closer, those dark eyes inquiring. "What has broken your heart?"

I shook my head, glad Gianni had returned with our antipasti—*cappesante, canestri, carote e lemongrass*—a delicious appetizer of scallops in cocoa butter and carrots puree with thyme and lemongrass. Gianni served as waiter and cook, describing each dish in loving detail.

"Delizioso!" Nico pronounced. I just moaned in response, closing my eyes in pleasure. Gianni went to serve another table, leaving us to fight over the rest of our antipasti, and we did—down to the last buttery bit.

"You are so sexy."

I smiled, dabbing my mouth with the napkin and lamenting the butter I lost on it. If it wouldn't have been impolite, I would have licked my finger. "Eating here is like having a food orgasm."

"Several," he agreed. "That was just the antipasti. We have primi, secondi, and dessert left to go."

"Dessert!" I groaned in anticipation. "You spoil me."

"You deserve to be spoiled."

"No." I took a sip of port and looked out the window where the sun was setting, melting into the water, turning it to liquid gold. "We humans aren't entitled to anything you know. Life is just a gift, not a promise."

"Agreed." He cocked his head at me. "And you're a gift to me."

"No," I countered again, but he leaned in to quell my protest and I let him, as if one kiss could wipe the slate clean and I could start over, right here, right now. For a moment, with his soft lips against mine, breathing in the musky, male scent of him, I thought it might be possible.

"Young love." Gianni put our primi course on the table. I blushed but Nico laughed, taking a bite of the *fettucini con ragout* and praising the chef's skill and presentation. Gianni beamed and went on to tell him about his technique, an artist talking about his work, while I took a heavenly bite of my own primi course, a perfectly cooked risotto with two types of clams.

Our secondi course was impossibly better than our primi. Nico's was a John Dory with a fava bean puree and turnip tops in chili pepper. He had ordered the *calamaro ripieno de patate* for me, knowing my love of seafood—squid stuffed with potatoes, prawns and scampi. Both were fresh, delicious, and meticulously and beautifully plated. The entire meal was an artful, luxurious experience, and I didn't think it could get any better—until Gianni brought dessert.

Nico ordered pistachio flan, which was fabulous, but for me there was a white chocolate and basil iced mousse and a sorbet made with green apple and wild fennel. I shared it reluctantly—I'd never tasted anything like it. Gianni received high praise from us both for the night and he asked us to come back, although I had a feeling we wouldn't be for a long while, considering the bill. I glimpsed it when Gianni brought it out along with a complimentary plate of cookies and chocolates and knew just how much Nico had spent on our extravagant dinner.

The evening was cool but we walked the streets anyway, holding hands and watching the sun set over Venice. It was probably the most romantic scene I'd ever stepped into—it could have been written in the pages of a book—and Nico's hand in mine made it perfection. If I'd learned anything in the past few years, it was to enjoy the moments, and this was one I knew I'd remember long after I'd departed Italy.

"I don't think I've ever had a meal quite like that," I admitted.

Nico smiled. "If you thought that was good, you should let me cook for you."

"I'd like that." I swung his hand, pondering. "Of course, that could prove a little difficult. There's no kitchen in my flat."

"We could use mine."

I hesitated before saying, "It's really your mother's, isn't it?"

"I live there too."

"Nico..." I sighed. "Do you ever want a place of your own?"

He didn't look at me. "It's complicated."

"I just wonder about a man who's twenty-five and still living at home with his mother." I knew immediately I shouldn't have said it, but it was exactly what I was thinking. And I think he knew it anyway.

"She needs me," he said simply.

"You could still help her, financially I mean, if you had a place of your own."

"But then I'd be paying rent somewhere, wouldn't I?"

"I suppose."

We turned a corner and I knew then where we were headed. My stomach fluttered and my limbs felt tingly. I wanted him—I always wanted him. It had become a constant.

"I think we feel differently about family in Italy than you do in America," Nico said.

I frowned. "What's that supposed to mean?"

"Perhaps we care more." The silence that followed his statement was telling to both of us. "That didn't sound right."

"Americans aren't all selfish and narcissistic you know," I reminded him stiffly.

"I didn't mean that."

"Yes you did."

He pulled me close, sliding his arms around my waist and bending his head to kiss me. I turned a little, deflecting, and he kissed my cheek, my ear, my neck, sending a white hot pulse through my veins.

"Come upstairs," he whispered, pressing his hand to the small of my back, letting me feel how much he wanted me.

"No." I shrugged out of his arms. "I don't want to get in your mother's way."

"Bella..." He reached for me again.

"Stop calling me that!" I backed away from him, hugging my arms across my chest. "Just... please stop calling me that."

"I don't understand you." He lifted his hands, helpless.

"That makes two of us."

He took another step toward me. "Please come up?"

I shook my head, feeling tears welling and fighting them. "I think maybe we need to spend some time apart."

"You're not making sense."

"I think I'm making perfect sense." I glanced up, seeing the square of light above where his mother was peering out, looking for us. "I can't be with a man who puts his family before me. I can't do that. Not again."

"Again?"

I turned away, blinking fast. I couldn't bear to explain. "It's a very long story, and I'm too tired to tell it tonight."

"You keep too many secrets." His hands squeezed my shoulders. "It's like a weight around your neck."

"You're probably right." I sighed, touching the charm at the end of the necklace Cara Lucia had given me. The eye of Beatrice, watching over me. "But they're mine to keep."

He murmured his words into my ear. "Sometimes you hold things so close to your heart that they crumble in your hands."

"Too late." I smiled. "The whole thing's already collapsed."

"We're talking in riddles."

I turned to face him, suddenly clear. "I think we just need to stop talking...for a while."

"Do you really mean this?"

"Yes." I nodded, telling myself I did mean it, that this was the right thing to do. I probably should have done it long ago. Beatrice would have been better letting him go, I reminded myself. Better for everyone.

He put his arms around my waist, bending his head to mine, reading my mind. "I won't let you go."

"You don't have a choice." I tried to disengage myself but he held me tight.

"Give me one."

I stopped struggling, meeting his gaze. "What do you mean?"

"Say you'll stay here in Italy." The urgency in his words made everything in me go silent. He was all seriousness, his eyes searching mine. "Stay with me. Give me a choice to make."

"Oh Nico..." I closed my eyes against the hope I saw on his face, filled with a pain I couldn't fight or control. "I'm sorry."

"Dani..." He said my name, soft, but he let me go.

And I walked home alone against the backdrop of a beautiful, blazing Venetian sunset, crying the whole way, feeling as if my life was fading away with the light, like an inferno in the sky.

Chapter Four

Dear Carrie and Doc,

You aren't going to believe who's showed up on my doorstep. I can barely believe it myself. Mason! That's right, I found my ex-husband sitting on my stoop, waiting for me after class, with just a suitcase and an English-Italian translation dictionary in his hands. I think I was too much in shock to do anything else but invite him inside.

And I swear to God, it's really not my fault he spent the night. He bought a one-way ticket and he didn't even book a room! What was I supposed to do, send him out onto the streets alone? He doesn't know a word of Italian—you should hear his accent, or lack thereof. Eek! But nothing happened. Well, mostly nothing.

Okay, okay, I admit, we, uh... we reconciled a little bit. Part of it was the wine. That was my fault. And, you guys, he brought me Ho-Hos! (No jokes, I mean it!) It's one of those weird, occasional indulgences of mine that I really miss. He knows me so well. It's hard to say no to a man who does something like that—not to mention the whole International flight to see me thing. But I think it was mostly the wine.

Of course, now this complicates things with Nico a bit. To say the least. I'm not sure what to say to him, if anything. And Mason says he wants to stay for a while, but I don't know what that means exactly. "Let's just see where things go," is what he said. I should have been mad at him, to tell you the truth. I should have slammed the door in his face and told him to go home. I mean, that's what I should have done, right? Isn't that what you would want me to do?

But I just couldn't. So now he's here, and I'm not quite sure what to do about that...

⟡⟡⟡⟡⟡

"Dani?" Mason's voice beckoned me back from the siren-call of Ho-Ho's in my little kitchen. I licked the chocolate off my fingers, tucking my letter to the Baumgartners away, and padded back into the bedroom, still nude. "What time is it?"

"Midnight." I sat on the edge of the bed, the little lamp on the night stand illuminating his sleepy face, eyes still half-closed—but his gaze was on my body, already hungry. Still hungry. "You're still on American time."

"Come back to bed." His hand moved, warm, over my hip, still familiar, even though it had been so long. I couldn't believe how easily I had fallen into bed with him, how easily I was falling... Maybe that thing about absence making the heart growing fonder really was true. Not that I had ever really stopped loving Mason. I'd divorced him knowing I would probably continue to love him for the rest of my life—but love didn't always solve everything.

"What are you doing here?" I murmured the question, running my hand through the soft, sandy bristle of his short-cut hair, so different from Nico's thick, dark curls. Thinking of Nico made my stomach lurch with guilt. I didn't want to think about what my actions tonight might be doing to him, to our budding relationship. It hurt my head—and my heart—too much.

"This." He reached for me and I went to him, relieved, without any more thought at all.

I couldn't believe how quickly we had plunged into this, how easy it felt, being in his arms. Sex had always been something we were good at, from the very beginning. At least until Isabella. Then, things had started falling apart and we just couldn't put it all back together again. That was probably why we'd ended up here, in bed, on his first night in Italy. We were good here. It was outside of bed that was the problem.

"I want you." His breath was hot in my ear, his hands large and warm, moving over my back, drawing me near.

"Again?" I teased, reaching down to check, and sure enough, finding him half-hard, beginning to fill my hand.

"Always." He kissed me, his mouth sliding deliciously across mine. Everything about him was familiar and new at the same time, and I reveled in it— the hard press of his chest, the solid weight of his hips as we rolled on the bed, the well-defined muscles of his arms and shoulders and back under my hands.

"I want to taste you."

I moaned in anticipation as he kissed his way down my breasts.

We'd been quick the first time, too quick, tearing at each other's clothes on the way to the bed, our lust too intense for niceties like foreplay. Seeing Mason sitting on the front stoop waiting for me had broken something open in my chest. A part of me that had been stuck and frozen solid was beginning to melt.

"God I love your tits." He pressed my breasts together in his big hands, getting my nipples as close as he could, and tracing figure-eights there like a skater on a loop, over and over. I whimpered, trying to stay quiet, my pussy throbbing, anticipating the wet lash of his tongue between my legs.

My belly quivered, goosebumps rising on my flesh as he breathed his way down my belly, pausing to lick the jut of my hipbone, following the curve down toward my thigh. I spread my legs for him, offering myself to him completely. I was his, I had always been his. How could I have ever believed any different? Time and distance, pain and separation, that all disappeared the moment his skin met mine.

"Oh God, it's so smooth." His fingers brushed my lips, soft and swollen, parting them at the top of my cleft so he could look at me. "So fucking beautiful."

I went up on my elbows so I could look down and watch. He smiled, knowing how much I loved to see his tongue lap at me, and began kissing my clit, soft, gentle kisses that sent electric shocks through my pelvis.

"Tease." I slid my palm over his head. His sandy hair was bristly and short—there was nothing to hold onto—so I slipped my hand behind his neck and pressed his mouth to my pussy. He didn't resist, letting me guide him, rocking my hips against the soft worry of his tongue, back and forth, round and round. "Oh God, yes, like that..."

But he knew. There was no need to tell him what I liked, what I didn't. His mouth knew just the right places, the exact timing I wanted, needed, moving faster, matching my breath. The excitement rose in my belly like a glorious phoenix from the ashes of a Persian mystery, something waiting to be reborn.

"Mason," I gasped, my fingers looking for something to hold onto and finding only the soft stubble of his hair. My nails dug into his shoulders and my hips shot up off the bed as my climax found me, zeroing in on my pelvis and shaking me like a kitten in the mouth of a pitbull. Mason hung onto my hips, licking my pussy fast and hard, holding me tight as I bucked on the mattress, biting the flesh of my forearm to keep from screaming in release.

"Oh fuck." I gasped, rolling away from his persistent mouth. He followed me, nipping at the soft curve of my ass, his hands roaming the length of my body as I stretched out on my tummy on the bed. I moaned into a pillow when he grabbed my hips, lifting my ass and using the head of his cock to search for entrance.

I clung to the sheet, my hands balling into fists as he found what he was looking for, rocking his hips forward and sliding his cock deep into me. I heard his sharp intake of breath, felt the way his fingers dug into my hips, and knew he was far closer to coming than he wanted to be. I smiled, closing my eyes and rhythmically squeezing the muscles of my pussy.

"Ohhh God," he moaned, his grip tightening. "You brat!"

"Feel good?" I teased, squeezing faster, harder, trying to mimic the hard flutter of my orgasm. He groaned in response, pulling out almost completely, leaving just the head of his cock at the opening of my pussy.

"Are you determined to make me come?"

"Eventually." I reached back to feel him, slick and hard.

"It's gonna be sooner rather than later if you keep that up."

My hand cupped his balls, rolling them gently. "Come all you want, we'll make more."

"Brat," he said again, slapping my ass and making me squeal. I giggled as he turned me onto my back, but then my mouth was too full to do much of anything else except suck his cock. He knelt over me and fed me his dick, inch by delicious inch. When I'd caught a good rhythm, he let his hips do the work, fucking my mouth, his thumbs grazing my nipples, making my pussy ache at the loss of his cock.

I gasped when he pulled out of my mouth, rubbing the head over my lips. They felt swollen and even a little numb, but I didn't care. I licked at the sensitive ridge of his cock, tracing the pulse of his veins, his dick so full it had turned magenta in color. I grabbed him in my hand, watching his face as I stroked him against my tits. His eyes lit up, a slow smile spreading.

"You want these?" I pressed my breasts together around his length, feeling his hips already beginning to move. "You want to fuck these pretty tits?"

"Spit on my dick," he ordered, shoving his cock up toward my mouth. I did as he requested, rubbing my saliva into the head and down into my cleavage. "Oh yeah. That's so fucking good!"

His cock rode the ridge of my breastbone, his hands cupping and kneading the flesh of my breasts as he began to fuck them. With each pass, I tried to capture the head of his cock with my mouth, eager to taste the pre-cum developing at the tip.

"You like having your tits fucked, don't you, baby?" He thumbed my nipples, sending heat down between my thighs.

"Yes," I admitted, wedging my hand under him, searching for my clit. It seemed so far away, but it was still begging to be touched. Finally, I reached my destination. God, I was wet. Soaked. My fingers followed the groove of my pussy like a Slip-N-Slide, up and down, as Mason used my tits for his pleasure.

The feel of him rocking my whole body, my nipples hard, my breasts squeezed tightly around his cock, made me crazy with lust. I rubbed my clit furiously, trying to catch up to him. He was panting, sweat beading on his chest, sheening his belly. I wanted to lick it off, tongue his navel, but couldn't reach. I could barely reach the head of his dick as it neared my mouth, but I put forth the effort, rewarded with a low growl every time I caught it between my lips.

"Where do you want me to come?" he panted, eyes half-closed.

"In my pussy," I insisted, plunging my own fingers into my hole, aching to feel his cock there. "Please. Fuck me. Do it, fuck me!"

He surprised me, rolling to his back and pulling me on top of him.

"Come on, Dani," he urged. "Ride me."

I found his cock trapped between us and slid down his length, sighing blissfully when I felt him bottom out. I rested there, just rocking, feeling him shift deep inside of me. He groaned, biting his lip, his thumbs digging into my hips as we began to rock together. I leaned over to kiss him, wanting more, sucking his tongue into my mouth.

We moved together in perfect rhythm. Mason's fingers found my clit, knowing just what I needed, flicking it faster and faster as we chased down the finish line like two race horses, panting and slick with sweat. I felt the first tremor of my climax beginning in my thighs. They tightened and quivered at his hips, his cock plunging deep into my pussy, his tongue into my mouth.

I couldn't stop it and didn't want to try. My pussy clamped down violently onto his cock, all sound receding as I came, the feeling so intense I had to break our kiss and bury my face into the crook of his neck, as if I could hide from the sensation. My toes curled under his thighs, my arms wrapping themselves around his neck as he pounded up into me like a jackhammer, making my teeth rattle.

"Gonna come," he growled, wrapping his arms around my waist and shoving himself up so far into me I thought I could taste him at the back of my throat. "Oh fuck, Dani, I'm gonna come inside you!"

I cried out at the brutal force of his orgasm, still recovering from my own, his hips lifting me off the bed, his cock convulsing wildly inside of me, filling me with heat. The strength of it left me breathless and I hung onto him, quivering with emotion, as we slowly came back down to some semblance of reality.

It was a while before I could think, let alone speak, but eventually my mind remembered what my body couldn't seem to hold onto. This was my ex-husband—and he was my ex for a reason. Many of them. And all of those reasons came flooding back, along with the memory of Nico the last time I'd seen him, leaving him standing at his front stoop, and I felt suddenly overwhelmed with it all.

"Mason?"

"Hmm?"

I traced his navel with my fingernail. "What are you doing here, really...?"

"I told you. I have business here."

I shook my head in disbelief. "In Italy?"

"I'm bringing the chain to Europe," he explained. His father owned a popular restaurant franchise in the states. I supposed it was plausible. But the Mason I had left back in the states had few ambitions aside from getting to the next level playing Dungeons and Dragons with his friends. Who was *this* Mason, the one who arrived in a business suit?

I laughed. "Just what Italy needs—hamburgers and fries."

"Listen, Ms. Ho-Ho..." He reached over to tickle me and I giggled, pushing his hands away. It was hard to stay serious—so hard to resist him.

"Who are you calling a ho?" I protested.

He kissed me hard on the lips, smiling down at me. "God, I missed you."

"I missed you too."

"Really?"

"Obviously. You wouldn't be in my bed right now if I hadn't missed you, Mason," I reminded him. "But I have bad news. You can't stay here. We're not supposed to members of the opposite sex in our rooms."

"That's okay," he said, pulling me close again. "I need to get my own place."

I raised my head to look at him in the dimness. Who was this man and what had he done with my husband? Er—*ex*-husband. "How long are you staying?"

"At least a month. I have to finalize plans here, find some prime real estate for our locations."

"A month." I blinked. When I'd left, I didn't think he was even on track to graduate, but here he was, talking business as if it was second nature. "You're really here just for business?"

"Well..." He cleared his throat and I waited, just looking at him. "Expanding into Europe was kind of my idea..." he admitted. "And... so was starting in Italy."

"So you came to see me." I would have denied the thrill that went through me at the thought, but it was there nonetheless.

"Is that bad?" He kissed the top of my head.

"No." I settled my cheek against his chest. "Yes... I don't know." I paused, thinking, and decided to just come out and ask. "What happened, Mason?"

"What do you mean?"

I hesitated. "When I left, you weren't too interested in much of anything, except hanging out with Darron and playing D&D. Now you're here in Italy talking about expanding your father's business. So... what happened?"

He was quiet for a moment, and then his arms tightened around me and he said, "I lost you. That's what happened."

I could barely breathe.

"You weren't the only one hurting you know," he reminded me, his voice low. "But you leaving... that was a wake-up call for me. At first, I tried to just keep doing what I'd always done. What my parents wanted me to do." He sounded angry, bitter. I winced. "But I couldn't. You took my whole world with you, and I had to get it back. At least, I had to try."

"How did you know I'd take you back?"

"I didn't." He chuckled. "I'm as surprised as you are that I'm here in your bed, you know."

"Are you?"

"I fully expected you to slam the door in my face."

I laughed. "And you came anyway?"

"Yes." His arms tightened around me.

I was thinking about Nico. Mason felt so good, familiar—comfortable. Being in his arms was like coming home. But what was I going to do? I couldn't just drop everything because Mason had come for me. Besides, the problems we'd always dealt with would resurface, I was sure of it. Why wouldn't they?

Unless Mason really had changed...

I sighed. "I just don't know how this is going to work."

"Let's just see where things go, okay?" His fingertips brushed over my arm and shoulder, making me shiver. "I'll be here. We can talk. Take it one day at a time. See what happens."

I shrugged, doubtful still. "If you say so."

"I also wanted to ask you a favor..."

"Uh-oh." I rolled my eyes. "Here we go."

"Doubting Thomas." He laughed. "Actually, I'd like to offer you a job."

"A... job?"

"I need an interpreter," he explained. "I'm going to hire one anyway, but I thought you might like the extra cash."

I half-sat, blinking at him. "Is this a bribe?"

"No strings attached, I promise." He crossed his heart. "Would you be willing to work with me?"

"I don't know." I frowned.

"Work on us?"

"Oh, Mason..." I snuggled up again, closing my eyes, wishing I could believe.

"Let's sleep on it." He kissed my forehead and that's just what we did.

"Phone." Mason nudged me but I was only half-awake. I buried my head under my pillow and snuggled more deeply under the covers. "Dani, phone."

It was only when he reached for it that I reacted, practically leaping over him to grab it. I fell onto the floor, still naked, shivering in the transition from warm covers to cold air.

"Hello?" I gasped, already dragging the phone on its long cord toward the bathroom.

"Morning, bella." The sound of Nico's voice made me flush and I closed the door behind me.

"Hi." I whispered.

"Did I wake you? It's almost noon."

"Is it?" I blinked at the sunlight streaming through my bathroom window. I'd been up far too late, and had been woken up, several times, in the middle of the night. Of course, I couldn't exactly tell him what I'd been doing, now could I?

"Are you sick?"

"No, I'm fine," I protested.

"You sound hoarse."

Of course I did. I was whispering. "I should go."

"But I want to talk to you."

Mason knocked on the door. "Dani?"

Oh crap.

"Later," I whispered, closing my eyes and praying for a miracle. "Meet me at the Mood Café in an hour."

I hung up the phone just as Mason knocked again, louder this time. "Dani, are you okay?"

"Fine!" I called brightly, standing and opening the door.

"Who was that?"

"I had a study group at noon," I lied. "They were wondering where I was."

"Why did you take the phone into the bathroom."

"I had to pee." I lied. "You know me, as soon as I get up, I have to go." In fact, I had to go now. "Listen, I have to hop in the shower and get ready to go. Will you be okay here for a few hours?"

He shrugged. "I'll just go get myself some lunch."

"Are you sure you'll be okay?"

"I've got my English/Italian dictionary, don't I?" He grinned. "And I can say *hamburger e patatine fritte.*"

I laughed. "That will get you a hamburger and fries."

"Then I'm all set."

I rushed through my shower, put on jeans and a t-shirt and grabbed my jacket, calling out to Mason, who was now in the shower himself, that I was leaving.

"I left a key on the table," I called, peeking behind the curtain. His hair was all soapy, and the sight of the suds dripping down his chest, over the flat, ridges muscles of his abdomen, made my breath catch. I didn't dare let my gaze dip lower.

"Thanks." He rinsed, rubbing his eyes and blinking at me. He saw the way I was looking at him and grinned. "Sure you can't stay a while?"

I thought of Nico waiting for me at the café and sighed. "Later. I'll be back in a few hours. Can you feed Jezebel?"

"Sure."

Nico was waiting already, although I was right on time. He smiled as I approached, rising to kiss my cheek and pull out my chair.

"Don't say anything." He held up a finger as I opened my mouth, which was probably a good thing, because I wasn't sure what I was going to say anyway. "I want to apologize."

I just sat and ordered a vanilla Coke, waiting for Nico to continue.

"You're right, this whole trying to find a place for us is crazy." He reached over and took my hand. "And you have become far more important to me than my mother or my family. I want you to know that."

"Nico..."

"No, wait." He turned my hand over in his, tracing the lines of my palm with his finger. "I'm going to look for a place. My own place. So we can stop this sneaking around."

I blinked at him, stunned. I probably would have jumped up and hugged him if he'd delivered this news a few days ago. Now I could just sit and stare, a growing pit of anxiety settling in my stomach.

"I..." What could I say? I'd come here with the intention of telling him about Mason. I knew I should tell him the whole story, my entire history, strip myself bare before him.

The waiter came and I sipped my Coke, grateful for the interruption. He asked if we wanted to order food, but Nico paid for our drinks, telling him no.

"I'm hungry," I protested.

"I have a surprise for you." He smiled, standing and reaching for my hand.

"Where are we going?"

The gondola was waiting and he helped me into it.

"Al Ponte Antico."

I stared at him. "The... hotel?"

"I rented a suite for the night."

"But..." I thought of Mason, waiting for me back at my flat. What in the hell was I going to do now?

"It's Saturday," he reminded me. "You don't have class."

"No..." I swallowed, trying to think of something, anything.

"And I'm taking the day off." He grinned down at me, triumphant. "Aren't you happy?"

"Yes." I bit my lip, seeing the glint in his eyes. "Of course I am."

And part of me was. The other part of me was panicking like a kid realizing their winter sled was hurtling downhill off a cliff.

The hotel was one of the most expensive in Venice and I knew he must have practically emptied his savings account to afford it. Nico remarked on my suddenly quiet demeanor, but the truth was, I was overwhelmed with guilt. How could I possibly tell him no? But if I didn't... what in the world was I going to do about Mason, back in my little room, with Cara Lucia patrolling the hallways?

"Do you want to eat first?" Nico offered, carrying a bag over his shoulder as we headed to the room.

Suddenly it occurred to me. "I don't have a change of clothes."

He smiled, taking out the key. "I took care of that."

"How?" I followed him down the hallway.

"I bought you a few things." He held up the bag as he worked the key in the door lock.

"Nico!" I blinked at him, still shocked by his revelation, and even more bowled over by the room when he opened the door. The suite was large, oriental rugs on the floors and a gold, ornate headboard over the huge bed. I couldn't help rushing to the window, the sweeping view of the Grand Canal breathtaking before us, as if we could just walk out onto the water.

"You belong here." Nico's breath against the nape of my neck made me shiver.

"In Al Ponte Antico?"

"In Italy." His arms went around my waist. "With me."

And I knew he was right. My whole life I'd dreamed of this, living in the city where the streets were made of water and the buildings held the secrets of an ancient history like a pent up breath. There was no more beautiful, vibrant, living place for me than Venice, and I couldn't imagine myself living anywhere else.

What was I going to do?

"Stay with me, Dani." Nico nuzzled me, his words melting my heart. "I can't live here without you anymore."

"Don't say that." I turned, twining my arms around his neck. "We hardly know each other..."

He shook his head, his smile knowing and telling at the same time. "We know everything we need to know. And you know it."

I did.

He kissed me, soft and slow and sweet, breathing me in. What girl could say no to him?

"I have something for you." He went to his bag and dug through, holding a brown package out to me. "My sister helped me gauge your size."

I looked at him, smiling. "What is it?"

"Something for you." He sat down in one of the chairs, looking up at me, slowly unzipping his jeans. "And for me..."

"You want me to open it?"

"Go to the bathroom and put it on."

I couldn't resist. It was the finest, silkiest, sexiest lingerie I'd ever seen, all black. The corset had straps on the bottom for the silk stockings, the thong was black with two straps across each side and there were even a pair of sexy black heels included—just my size.

I knew he was out there waiting for me, but I took the time to clean up a bit once I had stripped down. Then I tried it all on, looking at myself in the full-length mirror on the back of the door, my breasts pushed up by the corset, nipples pursed and hard, my legs long and shapely, the heels making them even moreso.

When I opened the door, I found Nico still sitting in the chair still mostly dressed, his cock out, hard in his hand, waiting for me. His eyes darkened as I approached, his gaze sweeping over me in the outfit he'd chosen.

"You like what you see?" I cocked one hip, my hand resting there, smiling down at him.

"You're beautiful," he said simply. "Turn around."

I did as he asked, turning in a full, slow circle, facing him again.

"Bellisimo." His cock was fisted tightly in his hand and just the sight of it made my knees weak. "I don't know if I should fuck you or eat you."

I grinned. "You can always do both."

"Good idea." He grabbed my hips, twisting me so my back was to him, using the flat of his hand to bend me forward. "Grab your ankles."

I did, the blood rushing to my head, making me dizzy, my long, dark hair grazing the floor.

"You like the shoes?" His hands roamed over my ass, snapping the thong, moving down the smooth silk stockings on my legs.

"Love them," I admitted, and from this angle, I had a great view. They were definitely Italian in design, and not cheap. "Nico, you spoil me."

"I've only just begun." His fingers moved my panties aside and he slipped his tongue between my pussy lips from behind, spreading my ass with his palms.

I gasped at the sensation, the sweet press of his mouth against my flesh so overwhelming I almost lost my balance. He steadied me, spreading my legs wider, his tongue plunging, tasting me deeply. My thighs quivered and I gripped my ankles more tightly, arching my back to give him better access. He chuckled, running his tongue up and down my slit, making me moan and wiggle back against him.

"Oh God, I'm gonna pass out."

"We can't have that." He pulled me back to sit in his lap, the teeth on the open zipper of his jeans biting my thighs, his hands tight on my hips. He rocked me against his cock. I could feel it pressed against the crack of my ass, riding along the string of the thong between my legs.

"You're going to put a run in my stockings."

He chuckled, reaching for the garter straps, undoing the front and then the back on my left leg, his hand sliding under the material, down the inside of my thigh. I shivered, closing my eyes, as his hand moved back up, cupping my mound and rocking me. His cock was so hard it felt like granite between us.

Then he undid the other one, his hand moving down the smooth expanse of my inner thigh to slide the stocking down, moving back up to nestle my mound in the palm of his hand. I turned my head and found his mouth, kissing him deeply, his tongue twining with mine. His hands moved up my waist, over the corset, fondling my breasts, our hips grinding in the chair.

"You're so beautiful," he gasped when we broke our kiss, looking down at me sprawled across his lap.

I lifted one of my legs, pulling my knee back so I could work the strap on my left shoe. It dropped to the floor and I slid the stocking down my calf. Then I did the other one, slowly sliding the stocking down to my ankle, Nico watching it the whole way. Then he stood me up again, this time turning me to face him, hands roaming over the length of my bare legs, up my hips to my breasts and back down again.

"Put the shoes back on."

I smiled, stepping back into them and buckling the straps, two on the outside of each high heel.

"Spread your legs."

I did, my hips jutting forward, watching his hand move up and down the length of his shaft as he looked up at me. His eyes were dark with lust, his lips slightly parted, so sexy sitting there with his jeans undone just enough for his cock to escape, his white button-down shirt untucked. I couldn't think about anything else except how much I wanted him.

"Touch yourself." His gaze fell between my legs to where the black triangle of the thong barely covered the swell of my bare pussy lips. "I want to watch."

I slipped my hand under the elastic, my pussy already wet from his tongue, slippery with my juices. I found the hard button of my clit with one hand, nudging it back and forth, watching his eyes light up as I traced my nipple with my fingernail, making it pucker. I teased my pussy, making my first two fingers into a V and letting them ride down around the nub of my clit, rubbing myself like that, my hips rocking.

"Let me see." Nico pulled the thong aside, biting his lip when he saw how my swollen pussy lips were parted for the press of my fingers. I slid the panties down to my ankles, stepping out of them, spreading my legs even wider this time. He groaned as I lifted my fingers to my mouth, licking my juices off them, sucking on them before sliding my hand back down to pay more attention to my pussy.

"Put your fingers inside," he said, his breath coming in short pants, his hand moving faster up and down the length of his cock.

I put one high heel up on the arm of his chair, giving him a full view. "You do it."

"Holy fuck." He said this in English, his eyes glazed with hunger, on eye-level with my pussy. He parted me with his fingers, working them slowly in and then out, watching himself finger me. I rolled my hips forward, giving him better access, my head going back, a low moan escaping my throat. He was incredibly skilled, thumbing my clit as he rocked his hand against my pussy, his fingers doing things inside of me that drove me crazy.

"Sit on my face, Dani." He pulled me toward him. "I have to taste you."

He positioned me, knees on the arm of the chair, hands gripping the back, his mouth covering my slippery mound. His tongue worked its way to my clit, his fingers finding their mark again inside of me, the other hand cupping my breast, thumbing my nipple, a trifecta of sensation. My thighs quivered, my belly undulating, coming so close to climax I could almost taste it.

"Please," I begged, my whole body tense, rocking. "Oh God, please! Please!"

Nico took me there, sucking my clit hard into his mouth, manipulating it with his tongue, making my pussy spasm in release around his plunging fingers. I cried out, my nails digging into the back of the chair, grinding my hips, shoving my whole pussy against his greedy mouth.

"Oh God!" I cried, shuddering still, sinking to the floor between his knees, now eye-level with his cock. I looked up to see his face glistening with my juices, his cock jutting up like a mast with no sail, waiting to be taken for a ride, and I couldn't resist. Still dazed from my own orgasm, I took him into my mouth, the head slick with precum.

His hand moved through my hair, guiding me up and down his length, his hips beginning to thrust in rhythm. I made soft, happy noises in my throat, my nipples grazing his jean-clad thighs as I took his cock between my lips again and again, feeling the thick length of him sliding against my tongue. My pussy was still throbbing for him. I couldn't believe how much he made me want him.

"I want you inside me." I slapped the head of his cock against my cheek, teasing the tip with my tongue. "Fuck me. Please."

"Your wish is my command," he said in English. "Stand up."

I did, and he stood with me, kissing me deeply, letting me taste my pussy on his tongue. Then he turned me around, pushing me further into the room. I thought he was taking me to the bed, but he walked me past it, toward the windows. They were covered by filmy white curtains, but he opened them, making me gasp and move to cover myself.

"I want the whole world to see you, bella," he whispered into my ear from behind me, his cock riding between the crack of my ass as he pressed me up against the window. The view of the Grand Canal was beautiful, the sun glinting off the water, a water-taxi passing by as I watched. I was topless, the corset pushing my breasts up against the window sill.

"You're crazy!" I gasped, but he threw the window open wide, and we both might have fallen out if it weren't for the railing between us and the wide waterway. I grasped it, crying out as Nico shoved his cock into me from behind, thrusting up hard. His hand grabbed my hips for leverage, fucking me hard and deep and fast.

"Wait!" I cried, but he wouldn't, and I couldn't do anything but hang on, my breasts swaying in the cool April breeze, knowing that anyone could see us. "Oh God, no, no..."

"You feel so good," he moaned, leaning over me, his pelvis molded to my ass, his cock buried to the hilt. "I'm going to come so hard inside of you."

I moaned and gave in to the sensation, my knuckles gripping the railing so hard they were white, going up on my tiptoes, even in heels, to take more of him, all of him, as deeply as I could. My pussy swallowed him up like it had been starving for him, as hungry as I was for his cock, his cum. I fucked him back, grinding my ass into the saddle of his hips, crying out, not caring anymore who heard us, who saw.

"Make me come all over your cock!" I panted, not daring to close my eyes, even as close as I was to climax. The water lapped at the cement below us, licking the sides of the seawall like a dirty wet tongue. "Oh fuck, fuck, I'm gonna come!"

He grunted and fucked me harder, deeper, a hand on my shoulder now for even better purchase. I could barely hold onto the railing, my back arched, my pussy stretched wide for the thrust of his cock. I was lost, gone, being fucked on the banks of the Grand Canal in Venice and about to have the most intense orgasm of my life.

And I almost said Mason's name.

It hovered on my lips, a low "Mmmmmmm" in my throat, and I kept it there, muffling my cries.

My climax hit like a shockwave, shuddering through me. If he hadn't had me around the waist with one arm, I would have collapsed to my knees. My pussy clamped down on his swollen length, the motion just enough to send him over with me. I rode the pleasure waves, letting them wash over me again and again.

"Oh my God," I gasped, feeling him slipping out of me, turning in his arms. He was grinning, panting, his eyes half closed, swinging the window shut and pulling me into his arms.

"You're so incredible." He kissed my cheek, my temple, my jaw, pulling me up so tight my feet left the floor. "I could eat you up."

"You're crazy." I was laughing now in his arms, my heart still beating like bird's wings in my chest. "You know that? You're just crazy."

"Crazy for you, yes." He kissed me and I could feel the smile still on his lips. "Are you glad I rented the room now?"

I glanced back at the window, not open now, but the curtains still open. I wondered how many people had seen us, if the hotel would get calls or complaints.

"I'm not sorry," I admitted, my weak knees finally giving out. I collapsed in the chair behind me, looking up at him with a half-smile.

"I'm glad." He slid his jeans down his hips and I raised an eyebrow. He laughed. "I'm just going to take a shower before we go eat. Unless you want to go again...?"

I groaned, shaking my head. "Not yet."

"But many more times," he promised, a hand moving through my hair. "Today, tonight, tomorrow..."

I smiled, but guilt twisted a knife in my belly and I gritted my teeth through the pain as Nico went to the bathroom. I looked down at my outfit, cold now, and shivered. All I could think of was Mason, waiting back at my flat. I'd left him there to come here with Nico and had spent God only knows how long having sex. Now how was I supposed to tell Mason I wasn't coming back tonight? Or how was I supposed to tell Nico I had to leave?

It was impossible.

I heard Nico turn on the shower and I ran over and flung myself across the bed, reaching for the telephone, knowing I didn't have long.

"Hey, there you are!" Mason's voice was warm and my body's temperature changed the moment I heard it. "I was starting to get worried."

"I'm sorry, I got caught up," I said, keeping my voice low.

"So, where do you want to go to dinner?"

"Well, the thing is..." I glanced toward the bathroom door and prayed Nico didn't open it. What was I going to say? How was I going to get out of this? It didn't occur to me that I should have had a plan before I picked up the phone to call.

"Are you okay?"

"I'm fine, I just..."

Then my worst nightmare came true.

Nico came out of the bathroom, fully nude, heading for his bag next to the bed when he noticed I had the phone in my hand.

"Who's that?" he inquired. "Room service?"

I could have covered the mouthpiece and lied, continued with the ruse, but I didn't have the heart—or the stomach—to do it anymore.

"Mason, I'll call you right back." I hung up the phone, looked at Nico, and told him the truth. "That was my ex-husband."

"Your...what?" He blinked at me.

"I'm sorry." I patted the bed, urging him to come sit. "I should have told you before."

He joined me on the bed. "But he's your *ex*-husband."

"Yes. We've been divorced for a year or so. But he's here in Italy. He came last night."

"Why?" His face said he already knew the answer, and so did I.

"He says he has business here, but I think..." I sighed. "The truth is, he wants me back."

"Bella..." He turned me toward him, his eyes soft, a little wet. I pretended not to notice. "I want you too."

"I know." I looked down at the carpet. "That's the problem." I stood, starting to dress. "I have to go."

"Please stay."

I found my panties and bra in the bathroom, my jeans in a ball on the floor. "I can't."

"Are you going to him?" he asked, watching me pull on my t-shirt, slip on my shoes.

"No..." I hesitated at the doorway, looking back at him. "I don't know. I just need to go somewhere to think for a while."

"I'll be here." He looked so sad, so vulnerable, just sitting there on the hotel room bed, that same bed he'd hoped we'd spend the night in. I thought the guilt couldn't get worse, and then he said, "I love you."

"I have to go." I pulled the door open and practically ran out.

Chapter Five

Dear Carrie and Doc,

I had to be honest with them both. You were so right. So I told Nico about Mason, and Mason about Nico, and now things are even more crazy than they were before. I guess some part of me expected one or the other of them to give me an ultimatum or just abandon me altogether once they found out I was seeing them both, but it seems as if my life just wants to be complicated.

"We're not married anymore. I have no claim over you. Just hope, Dani. That's all I have." That's what Mason said to me when I told him I'd been seeing someone else. But you're not going to believe what else he said. "I just want to prove to you that you can trust me. I love you, and I hope that you can give our relationship another chance."

Of course, Mason always talked a good game. But the thing is, this time... he's actually backing his words up with reality. I know he's here on trust fund money and all—his parents' money—but he's also here in direct defiance of everything they wanted for him. His father didn't want him to come here, didn't want to take his part of the business overseas. They, of course, had hoped he'd forgotten about me entirely. But he's here, he says he's still in love with me, and that he wants to work things out. And for once, I believe him.

But then there's Nico. I can't say if I'm in love with him or not. Things are still so new. But I think... I think I am. We had a fight the other day about—of all things—his mother. (Why do I keep picking men with mother issues? Never mind, I bet I don't want to know...) Anyway, I felt awful afterward, and I realized, after two days of not talking to him, how much I really, really missed him in my life, how much I'd started counting on him to be there for me.

I feel so torn now. And Nico was just as accommodating as Mason, for pete's sake, when I told him. "Whatever you want." That's what he said. "I'll accept whatever makes you happy." So for now, I'm dating them both. Which is strange and awkward— they've met now and seem to loathe each other, which I guess is understandable—and I know I'm going to have to make a choice at some point in the near future.

I just don't know what I'm going to do. Maybe I should run away to Michigan and come live with you guys? Ha ha. (Only kind of kidding...)

❦

"How can you both live in the same place?" Bewildered, I looked between Mason and Nico, both of them standing in the kitchen of the apartment, their arms crossed, identical scowls on their faces.

"We've come to a truce," Nico explained, speaking English out of courtesy to Mason. "It's the only one left in the building, and it has two bedrooms."

I gaped at him. "Roommates? You're going to be roommates?"

"Why not?" Mason shrugged. "It's cheaper. And they're willing to sign a month to month lease, which is something I haven't been able to find anywhere else in this city."

"But... but..." I couldn't even begin to tell them how much of a bad idea I thought it was. I sputtered and spat my objections, which just came out as garbled gibberish.

"It will be easier for you," Nico remarked with a smirk. I could have smacked it off his face.

Mason snorted a laugh. "True enough."

"This is crazy," I muttered, storming off toward the bathroom. It was hard enough, being with both of them at once, especially since they turned everything into some sort of pissing contest. But having them live together? It was impossible. I splashed water on my face, frowning into the little mirror over the sink.

And then it occurred to me. Maybe this was part of their plan. If I couldn't separate them, split them up, see one here and one there, I'd have to make a choice faster, wouldn't I? But then what? What happened when I chose Mason instead of Nico? Or Nico instead of Mason? Both scenarios made me feel dizzy and I gripped the edge of the sink, breathing hard.

"Dani?" It was Mason, knocking.

And then there was Nico, right behind him, echoing, "Dani? Are you all right?"

"Fine!" I called, opening the door to find them both standing in the doorway. I sighed, looking between the two of them. "So now what?"

"Now we buy furniture," Mason replied, slapping Nico on the shoulder. "We've already got beds though, right?"

I blinked. "You do?"

"Mine from home," Nico explained. "And my sister gave us another. I put it in the second bedroom."

"My room," Mason reminded him.

"She's okay with this?" I scoffed.

Nico looked sheepish. "I told her it was for a friend."

"And what does your mother say about it?" I inquired.

His jaw tightened. "It doesn't matter. I'm moving out."

"Good for you, man." Mason slapped him on the shoulder again.

"Am I in a *Twilight Zone* episode?" I asked faintly, shaking my head.

Mason turned to me, putting his hands on my shoulders. "Hey, I've got a meeting tomorrow afternoon. Can you come as my interpreter?"

Nico scowled. "We were supposed to go to the gallery tomorrow afternoon."

"We can do the gallery after the meeting," I said to Nico.

"I suppose." His scowl disappeared when he said, "Oh, my sister wanted to know if you could come to dinner at her place tonight."

I bit my lip "Is it something special?"

"It's Maria's tenth birthday." Anna's daughter. I knew she'd be disappointed if I didn't show up.

"We're going to dinner tonight," Mason reminded me.

I sighed. "I did already make plans."

Nico relented, but tried again. "What about tomorrow night?"

"How many birthdays does your niece have?" Mason countered.

Nico rolled his eyes. "Very funny."

"I could do dinner with you tomorrow night," I offered, trying to make peace. This was impossible.

"We can go to *Il Ridotto* again."

I shook my head and sighed. "Nico, that's so expensive."

"That's where I'm taking her," Mason interrupted. "I don't think she's going to want the same thing two nights in a row."

The irony of that statement didn't escape any of us.

"I think *Il Ridotto* once a year is sufficient," I said.

Nico didn't give up. "There's always the *Jazz Club 900*. Or we could go to another club. Do you want to go dancing?"

"Dani doesn't dance." Mason snorted laughter.

"I dance!" I nudged him with my elbow, admitting, "I just don't dance well."

"I can teach you." Nico took me in his arms and I saw Mason scowl as he led me lightly around the living room floor. "It's easy. You just have to let yourself go."

"Yeah, well, you can let her go right now." Mason stepped in, separating us, and the two men faced each other, glowering.

I smirked. "This living together thing is going to work well. I can tell already."

They both backed off a little, turning their glares toward me, saying almost simultaneously, "It will be fine."

"Oh!" I grabbed for something, suddenly lightheaded, and Mason caught me with an arm around my waist. Not to be outdone, Nico appeared on my other side, both of them buoying me up. "Dizzy. Too much dancing I guess."

"You should sit." Nico said, but there was no chair or sofa. The only furniture was the mattress in the bedroom and I wasn't even going to consider that, with both of them standing beside me.

"I have to go anyway." I untangled myself. "I have some studying I've neglected."

"I'll take you home." Nico offered.

"In the gondola?' Mason snorted.

Nico swiped his hand under his chin at Mason, the Italian equivalent to giving him the middle finger. *"Vaffanculo!"*

Mason didn't need an English to Italian dictionary to interpret what he meant.

"I'll walk," I said, heading for the door. "The fresh air will do me good."

"I'll see you tonight," Mason called. "Pick you up at seven?"

I didn't answer him. My flat was half a mile away, and it was good to be out in the fresh air. I gulped it down, trying to clear my head. Days like today, I was ready to tell both men to go jump in the Grand Canal and be done with it. Of course, when it came down to it, this thing was my own fault. If I would just make a decision, they would stop trying to compete with each other, right? So what was wrong with me?

I still couldn't believe the two of them had decided to room together. It made me wonder what they were up to. It was the last thing I'd expected, after my confession to first Nico and then Mason, that I was seeing them both. Part of me had expected Nico to end things, and Mason to turn around and head back to the states, but neither of those things had happened.

Jezebel mewed at the door when I opened it, demanding to be fed. I filled her bowl, glancing at the books on my little kitchen table. I'd been too distracted lately, first Nico and now Mason, neglecting my studies. I should have cracked the books but instead I poured myself a glass of wine and took it to the sofa, sitting and sipping and listening to Jezebel eat.

I couldn't get either man out of my head, and now I couldn't separate them either. When I closed my eyes and imagined them, their hands and mouths and voices melded in my mind. The wine, of course, wasn't helping. It made everything fuzzy around the edges. Jezebel joined me on the couch, kneading my thigh with her paws before settling next to me with a large yawn.

The knock on my door startled us both, and Jezebel followed me, just as curious as I was who might be calling. Cara Lucia stood there in the entrance, frowning, her gray hair covered, as usual, under a dark-colored scarf. She remained in mourning for her husband, who made it through WWII in one piece only to die twenty years later from delayed effects of nerve gas.

"Here." She spoke English, handing me a sheet of paper, and my heart dropped to my toes. Had someone seen Mason here and said something? Was I being evicted? "No more visitors in the room. *Capice?*"

Sure enough, it was a warning about having Mason over. Someone must have seen him coming or going. I cringed, folding the paper and putting it into my back pocket, already apologizing, but she waved my excuses away.

"I can't have different rules for different tenants." She was back to speaking Italian again. "I'm sorry."

"I understand." Of course I did. But I also knew she must be angry with me. I hadn't been to lunch with her since I started dating Nico. "I promise, no more."

"So this Mason, he's come for you?"

"I'm not sure why he's come." I nudged Jezebel back in. Thankfully the rules about pets were far more lax than her rules about men.

Cara Lucia smiled knowingly. "And what about this other one? The dark-haired Italian boy?"

Who did I think I was kidding? She didn't miss anything.

"We're..." What were we exactly? "We're working things out."

"Well don't take too long."

I frowned. "What does that mean?"

"You want a marriage. Babies. You're not getting younger, you know."

I jutted my chin out. "How do you know I want that?"

"You do." She scoffed. "The way you covet your friend's baby? Look at the pictures you have of her. You want what she has. I know you do."

I swallowed, thinking about Carrie and Doc and their little Janie. Did I want what they had? Some part of me did. And another part of me was scared to death of it. Some echo of a memory cried out, "Not again, never again." And then my body betrayed me, every single time I was with one man or the other.

"So consider this your first warning, yes?" Her eyes met mine. "No more visitors."

"You don't have to worry," I assured her, although I didn't explain that both Nico and Mason had found their own place—together. It was too weird, even for me.

"Good." She nodded her head, satisfied. She turned to go and then turned back, looking like she wanted to say something. "Are you all right?"

"Fine," I replied, attempting a smile, but I felt dizzy with my own realization. Did I want what she claimed I wanted? A husband? A child? A family? "I'm sorry about the...visitors. It won't happen again."

"Good." She hesitated again. "I think those boys are taking too much out of you. Maybe you should lie down. Get some rest. You look pale."

"I will." I pushed Jezebel out of the way again and shut the door, leaning against it for a moment, my head swimming. I was going to read and work on my thesis, but when I got the couch, Cara Lucia's suggestion was too powerful and my thoughts far too overwhelming. I fell asleep with Jezebel curled on my lap.

"This is too weird." I glanced at the bedroom door as Mason closed it behind him. The bed was the only thing in the room, so I sat there. They still hadn't purchased much in the way of furniture. There was a kitchen table now but no chairs, and a coffee table and a television in the living room. "Where's Nico?"

"He had to go help a guy with a leaky pipe." Mason grinned. "At least, that's what he said."

I rolled my eyes. "Was it Sal? His sister's husband?"

"I don't care." He came to sit next to me on the bed, his hand already moving up my knee, under my skirt. "I'm just glad we have the place all to ourselves."

"Still, if he comes home..."

"I locked the door." Mason captured my mouth with his, insistent.

Our dinner had been good—it was hard to get a bad meal in Venice—and our conversation even better. But both of us had been impatient for time alone. Every time our hands touched or our eyes met or my knee brushed his under the little café table, a spark of electricity passed between us, a surge of desire. I was already wet for him, had been for hours. And he knew it.

During dinner, he had leaned over and whispered, "Go to the bathroom and take your panties off."

And I'd done just as he asked, passing them under the table into his hands, letting him feel how moist they were, still warm from my pussy. His eyes had darkened with lust when he took them from me and slipped them into his suit coat pocket. It hadn't been long after that we were alone in a water-taxi heading, so eager for each other his hand had found its way under my skirt to my bare pussy, flicking my clit, teasing me as we sailed toward home.

We were just as eager now, his hands roaming over my blouse, pushing my skirt up to my hips, my aching clit finally getting his full attention. He rubbed it with his thumb as he kissed me down onto the bed, undoing the button of my blouse with his other hand.

Not to be outdone, I peeled his suit coat off, working the buttons on his shirt too. I was still getting used to Mason all dressed up in suits. The husband I'd been married to wore the typical college uniform— jeans and a t-shirt. I found this new Mason irresistibly sexy. It was the same man but different, and the change was exciting.

"God, I love your tits," he groaned, finally reaching his destination, undoing the front hook of my bra and letting them spill out. He grabbed them in both hands, his knee going between my legs so I could rub myself against his thigh. His tongue made circles around my nipples, tracing delicious patterns over my skin from one breast to the other.

"Mason," I whispered, arching my back, my pussy swollen against the press of his leg between mine. I could barely wait, my whole body pulsing with need. "I want your mouth. Please. Lick me."

He didn't need to be asked twice. I was hanging half off the edge of the bed, my legs dangling, and he got down on his knees on the floor, shoving my skirt up to my waist. I parted my pussy my lips with my fingers for him as he kissed his way up my thigh, his breath hot, fast. He was excited as I was.

He pressed my thighs open wider with his palms flat, shoving my legs back, rocking my hips up, completely exposing my pussy and ass to him. I moaned in anticipation, rubbing the hood of my clit with one finger, not wanting to wait. Mason was busy licking the inside of my thigh, following the fleshy seam between my leg and my pelvis with his tongue.

"You've got such gorgeous legs." He praised me, murmuring, in between kisses. He had them pressed far back, my heels still on. I didn't tell him they were the same heels Nico had bought me for our hotel stay. "Your skin is like silk."

"Please," I whimpered. Not that I minded the compliments. They made me flush with pleasure. I loved the way he looked at me, so wolfish, like he could put me in a dish and eat me with a spoon. Finally, oh God, finally his mouth reached my pussy, his tongue lapping up and down my lips, teasing the swollen, wet flesh, making me squirm on the bed.

"Oh my God, you taste so good." His tongue slipped through my cleft, smooth and slick, scooping up my juices as he went, spreading them over my labia, up to my clit. My hips lifted toward him in response the moment his mouth covered my pussy. He knew just what I liked, finding my pleasure center, that electric hot spot that made me quiver, feeling his way.

I'd forgotten how good he was, how well he knew me. My body responded without thought, giving myself to him like an offering, spread out and trembling. His mouth worked between my legs, but he kept his fingers busy too, working them slowly into my pussy, then moving them in and out, fucking me gently while he licked me.

"Oh God, baby, faster," I panted, grabbing my own knees, pulling them back. "Fuck me harder!"

He plunged his fingers into me, jolting my whole pelvis with a heart-pounding rhythm, his tongue never wavering on my clit. I was so close to orgasm, breathless and out of control, I felt full of heat and light, as if my whole body was on fire.

Then he slid a finger down and rubbing my ass, teasing the tight ring of my asshole, my juices and his saliva already making it wet. I gasped when he slid it in to the first knuckle, the sensation so naughty and at the same time so exciting it nearly sent me screaming over the edge toward orgasm.

"You like that?" he teased, knowing full well that I did. His fingers moved in deeper, then deeper still. He had a finger in each hole, pussy and ass, fucking me again gently. I thrust against his hand. Being fingered just made me want his cock and I found myself wishing he had more than one, so he could do me like this, just like this.

"Make me come." I pressed my hand to his head, fitting his mouth over my mound. "Lick it. Oh God, yes, like that. Please, please, make me come!"

His tongue found that spot again, working it with a vengeance as he fingered my pussy and my ass together, sinking deeper with every thrust. I cried out, digging my heels into his shoulders, my back arching as I came, my climax surprising us both with its force, my pussy and ass spasming together around his fingers in ecstatic rhythm.

Mason slid up between my thighs and I wrapped my legs around him as we kissed. I sucked at his tongue, tasting the musk of my pussy, feeling him fumbling with his belt and zipper. Then, oh then, his cock slid through the wet pleat of my pussy, seeking entrance. He groaned when he found what he was looking for, plunging into my wetness, not waiting, not giving me even a moment to breathe.

"Oh God!" I clung to him, the bed squeaking under our weight, Mason stretched out half on and half off, his feet on the floor, giving him greater leverage as he thrust. His shirt was open, his belly exposed as he rose above me like a God, blotting out the light. "Oh baby, no, wait, ohhhh! That's so fucking good!"

He grunted in response, rolling his hips, making circles against my pelvis, his cock taking inventory of my pussy, every last little bit of flesh explored. My orgasm was still fading, my body shivering under his weight. I felt his cock swelling inside of me, impossible proportions, filling me with every buck of his hips.

Then he slowed, panting in my ear, his muscles tense, his bottom lip pulled between his teeth.

"Mason?" I whispered.

"I want you to suck it." He rolled off me to the bed, onto his back, looking over at me. "Lick all your juices off my cock. Oh God, yeah, that's a good girl..."

I was up on my hands and knees, still dizzy from my climax but eager to give as good as I'd received. His cock was thick in my hand, throbbing as I took him between my lips, the head swollen. He moaned and grabbed a fist full of my hair, pushing me down, down, down, making me take him, every inch.

I gagged and he let me come up for air, but then it was back down again, his cock searching for my tonsils, seeking the hottest, fleshiest, deepest recesses of my throat. I gagged again, again, my eyes watering, but I loved it—and he knew it. He fucked my face like that, giving me his cock over and over, his thigh muscles taut, toes curled. I knew he was fighting climax, but enjoying it too much to stop me.

I cried out when he swung my hips around on the bed toward him, plunging his fingers back into my pussy, He worked them into my sopping wetness and back out again, twisting as he went. I arched my back like a cat stretching, still focused on his cock— although not quite so intently now. His thumb rubbed at the sensitive button of me clit, giving me even more cause to slow down on sucking him, my tongue pausing to roll around the ridged, mushroom head.

"Come here." He grabbed my ass, yanking me across him, positioning my pussy over his face and wrapping his arms around my hips. I whimpered but gave in to what he wanted, his tongue burying itself in my flesh, fucking my hole in and out, like a tiny cock. It was such a tease and I moaned around the fleshy thrust of the real thing in my mouth, aching for it to fill me.

"I want you," I begged, yanking his pants and boxers down his thighs for better access. I wrapped him in my fist, my tongue working down toward his balls, breathing in the pungent, masculine scent of him. "Oh God, I want your cock in me."

"Nuh-uh," he panted, taking a breath. "Not until you come."

"Again?" I squeaked in protest when his tongue found my clit, nudging it back and forth.

"At least twice."

I groaned, pressing my forehead against the meat of his thigh, his tongue dancing delightfully through the slick folds of my flesh. I stroked him absently in my hand, feeling precum building at the tip of his cock, too lost in sensation to do much else. When he made his tongue flat, pulsing it against my clit, I squeezed him so hard the head turned from red to purple above my fist, my breath coming so fast I could barely keep up.

"Mason! Baby!" I cried, biting at the soft flesh of his thigh. "Oh God I'm gonna come!"

He just grunted his encouragement, his tongue moving faster between my legs, his whole face buried between them. My climax shook me violently, the bed vibrating beneath us as I bucked on top of him, half sitting, forgetting entirely about his cock, my hands clenched into fists on his belly as I mashed the flesh of my pussy against his face, drowning him in sticky sweetness.

"Oh fuck." He nibbled at my pussy and thighs, breathing hard. "That was so hot I almost came with you."

"I forgot about your poor cock." I kissed the tip, tasting his precum.

"Well we're going to remedy that." He rolled me onto my back, making me squeal. My skirt and heels were still on, my shirt open, my breasts exposed. He undressed me quickly.

"I thought you were gonna make me come again?" I teased, lifting my hips so he could slide my skirt down my thighs. He dropped it on the floor with the rest of my clothes, leaving me completely naked.

"I'm gonna make you come again." He pulled his shirt off, kicking his pants and boxers free. "When I fuck your ass."

My eyes widened, my words gone, as he turned me over onto my belly, lifting my behind in the air. He smacked it, making me yelp, and rubbed his cock through my soaking wet crevice.

"Mason, wait," I begged, but there was no talking to him once he was determined he wanted something—and he wanted my ass.

It wasn't that we hadn't done it before. We'd experimented a lot during our marriage, and I'd had my ass taken quite a bit when I was with the Baumgartners. It was just that I wasn't ready for it, hadn't mentally prepared myself. It took an adjustment to go from wanting to be fucked, to wanting to be fucked *there.*

But I was going to have to get used to the idea pretty quick, if the way Mason was probing between my ass cheeks was any indication.

"You're so *wet,*" he exclaimed, his cock head pressed right against the tight entrance of my ass. I gasped, fisting the covers on his bed and burying my face there.

"Not yet," I begged again. "Please."

"Okay." His cock slid down to my pussy, thrusting in deep at this angle. I cried out, shifting my weight on the bed to take him so far in it almost hurt. "God that's hot. I love watching my cock go into you."

His finger circled the ring of my asshole as he fucked me, the wet slap of my wet pussy taking his length filling the room. My breasts swayed with the motion, my nipples grazing the bed. I caught his rhythm, rocking against him, fucking him back. He slid his finger into my ass, making me whimper and grind.

He knew I loved it, and we both knew what he was doing—priming the pump, so to speak.

"Feel good, baby?" He fucked my pussy and my ass, shoving both his cock and his finger in as far as they would go.

"Y-y-y-yes," I managed, his hips rocking me hard on the bed, shaking everything.

"You want it in your ass, don't you?"

Oh God, another finger. He wedged them both in, stretching me open. His cock was swollen to bursting inside of me. I felt the pressure inside, so full, both orifices stretched.

"Y-y-y-yes!" I said again, putting my shoulders down onto the bed and reaching back with both hands. I spread my ass cheeks open for him, hearing his sharp intake of breath. "Take it, baby. Fuck my ass."

He groaned at my permission, his dick slipping out, his fingers too, leaving me with a feeling of emptiness that was short-lived. His cock was dripping oil from my pussy like a dipstick out of a hot engine and I felt the press of it against the rigid muscle of my anus. I took a deep breath, determined to take him, closing my eyes and trying to relax.

"Oh fuck," he moaned, shifting on the bed to press in a little deeper. "So *tight.*"

My thighs trembled as he thrust again, driving himself in past that tight ring of muscle. I yelped in surprise at the burn, but he waited a moment and I recovered, moving my hips back toward his. He gripped my ass, settling himself in deep. I slid my hand between my legs, searching for the throbbing bud of my clit. I wanted to come like this, with him buried in my ass. How had he known just what I'd wanted—even when I didn't know?

"Fuck me," I begged, rolling my hips. "Fuck my ass 'til I come."

He pulled back, like loading a spring, and then we were off. I couldn't think, I couldn't breathe, I couldn't do anything but take him, again and again and again, the rising tide of my orgasm driven by the rock and thrust of his hips. His cock was a piston, urging me on.

"Mason!" I was so close. So very close.

"Come," he panted, his fingers digging into the sides of my hips. "Oh God, Dani, I can't hold back. I'm gonna come in your tight little ass!"

That did it. I was flying, his cock flooding me with cum, fountains of it, a geyser of lava deep inside of me. My pussy contracted again and again, my asshole clamping around his cock and he clung to me as if the force of it might drive him right out. But I wasn't letting him go. When he tried to pull out, I clenched my still-spasming muscles around the head of his dick, making him squirm and gasp.

"Easy!" he cried.

I smiled as he slid slowly out, feeling the "pop" of my flesh as my ass finally gave up. He crawled up next to me on the bed, pushing my hair out of my face and finding my cheek, kissing it. His breath was still hot and panting. So was mine. I floated, in a dream, until the sound of someone in the flat upstairs brought my head up off the bed.

"I should go."

His head came up too. "So soon?"

"I don't want to be here when Nico comes home." This reminded us both and we were silent for a moment, coming back down to reality. "This is all so strange." I sighed. "Why are you so quiet?"

"We agreed we wouldn't push you."

I rolled over on my side, up on my elbow to look at him. "We?"

"Me and Nico."

I blinked. "You've talked about this?"

"Of course we have."

He made it sound so matter-of-fact.

"How very civilized of you."

"This is your choice, Dani," Mason said softly, rolling toward me so we were belly to belly. "And we agreed that you needed to make it without our influence."

I frowned. "How can either of you not influence me?"

"I guess the gentlemen's agreement here is that we won't play dirty," he replied. "No bribes, no proposals, no promises. We just have to be ourselves and you... you have to decide which one of us you want."

I rolled away from him, to my back, throwing an arm over my head and staring at the ceiling.

"What is it?" he asked.

It sounded ridiculous, even as I said it—but it was the way I felt. "Aren't either of you going to fight for me?"

He chuckled. "Do you want us to?"

"Oh I don't know." I sighed, sitting up and searching for my clothes.

"I would." Mason sat too, watching me get dressed. "Put me in a cage with him. We'll fight to the death. Or perhaps you'd prefer jousting? Or Russian Roulette?"

"Very funny." I slipped my bra on, doing up the hook in front. "This is impossible."

"No it's not." He watched as I pulled on my blouse, working the buttons. "It's just a decision. Me or him."

"I thought you weren't supposed to pressure me?" I snapped, sliding my skirt up my hips and reaching around, trying to work my zipper.

"Am I?"

I stopped. "Mason, I'm afraid."

"Come here." He turned me around so he could zip my skirt. "Of what?"

"If I choose you..." I glanced back over my shoulder at him. "Well, we didn't get divorced for no reason, you know."

He smiled. "Yes, I know."

"Are we just going to pick up where we left off?" I turned in his arms, trying to see the truth in his eyes.

"No," he assured me. "I'm different. You're different."

"You're still so tied to your family." I sighed. "This is your father's business you're talking about, not your own."

"But I'm making my own decisions." He looked at my blouse, frowning, and started rebuttoning it. I'd missed one. "Trust me, they didn't want me to come here. They still don't want me to be with you."

"No?" I imagined that was true. They'd never liked me. I was a bad influence on their son.

"But this is me, making my own decisions." He looked up at me, his eyes serious. "I choose you. I want you. That's why I'm here."

I smiled. "I knew it wasn't just business."

"Hardly." He pulled me down into his lap and I straddled him as he kissed me, slow and deep, the smell of our sex redolent in the room. I'd missed us together, so much. Thinking about it brought tears to my eyes.

"What about Isabella?" I asked, swallowing past the obstruction in my throat.

"What about her?"

I blinked back tears. "Don't you miss her?"

"Of course I do." His arms tightened around me. "She was my daughter too."

I closed my eyes, feeling tears slipping down my cheeks. "I don't know if I'll ever get over it."

"I don't know if you're supposed to." Mason cupped my face in his hands, using his thumbs to wipe my tears. "But that doesn't mean we can't move forward."

"Oh God, please don't talk about more babies," I groaned, trying to twist away from him. "Not that again."

"Us, Dani." He turned my face to him again, meeting my eyes. "*We* can move forward, you and I, together. Babies can be a part of that or not. But I want you. *You.*"

I contemplated the idea. "What would we do?"

"Anything you want." He smiled, wrapping his arms back around my waist. "You'll be done with school in June. You can find a job here in Italy. Work here, stay here. Isn't that what you always wanted?"

I laughed, shaking my head. "You don't know a word of Italian."

"I'll learn." He nuzzled my belly, rested his head against my breasts. "Ti amo."

I love you.

I looked down at him in wonder, running my hand through his short-cropped hair.

"See, I'm already learning." He grinned up at me.

"It sounds too good to be true," I murmured. "What would you do?"

"I've got the business," he reminded me. "In spite of my father's reservations, I think branching out all over Europe is a brilliant idea, even if it is mine. And I think it's going to be very lucrative."

"I can't believe this is you talking," I said doubtfully. "I can't believe it's real."

"It's me. I'm real." His eyes told me everything I wanted to know. "And I do love you."

"I love you too," I whispered, kissing him softly. "I always have."

I slid off his lap, heading for the door.

"Where are you going?" he called.

"To pee." I stopped in the doorway, suddenly dizzy, leaning against the wall.

"Are you all right?"

I nodded, opening the door. "Just overwhelmed."

"Hurry back," he called. "I want your ass one more time before you go."

I grinned over my shoulder at him. "You are a bad, bad man."

"I know. Hurry back."

"Can you see yourself doing this for the rest of your life?" I asked, watching Nico navigate the gondola through the narrow passageway.

"Being with you?"

I smiled. "No, being a gondolier."

"Honestly?" Nico looked across the water, his hat shading his eyes. "No."

I sat forward in my seat. "So what do you want to do?"

He hesitated. "You'll laugh."

"No I won't," I assured him. "I promise. If you tell me... I'll tell you something. Quid pro quo."

"A secret?" Nico slowed the gondola, wrapping a rope around a nearby post.

"Yes."

"I want to be a chef," he confessed, stepping off onto the dock, reaching for my hand and helping me up. "I want to own my own restaurant, like Gianni Bonaccorsi."

His response thrilled me. "You'd be a wonderful chef."

"Do you mean that?" He took my hand as we walked the cobblestone toward the flat he was sharing with Mason.

"Of course I do."

He looked down at me, speculative. "I've been saving a long time to open my own restaurant."

"You should do it." I squeezed his hand.

He sighed. "It's hard to do something like that and still pay the bills in the meantime."

"But if it's your dream, you should do it anyway," I urged as we took the stairs in his building up.

Nico unlocked the door, changing the subject. "So tell me a secret."

"Is Mason home?" I asked, hesitating in the doorway. He'd already told me he wouldn't be there, but I wanted to be sure.

"No." He tossed his keys on the table. They had a flat full of furniture now. "He had business. And we have an understanding."

"Do you tie a sock on the doorknob?"

He laughed, reaching for me. "So tell me something."

"I'm a man in a woman's body," I confessed, putting my arms around his neck.

"Now I know that isn't true."

"I'm a woman who wants a man's body," I murmured, pressing my breasts against his chest.

"Well, that I believe." He smiled, his eyes lighting up. "But you're not getting out of it so easily. Tell me something real."

"Something real..." I pulled away from him, wandering around the flat. Mason had come with practically nothing, so the apartment spoke more of Nico's tastes, which meant a more classic Italian design. "I can't think of anything."

"You promised," he reminded me, taking my hand and leading me to the sofa. "You're such a mystery."

"You want to know something real about me?" I asked, letting him pull me onto his lap.

"Yes."

"Okay..." I took a deep breath and closed my eyes. "I had a baby. With Mason."

He was quiet for so long I had to look.

"And where is this baby?" he finally asked.

"She's..." I blinked fast, looking away, and whispered the word. "Dead."

"Ah bella..." He took a deep breath, taking my hand in his. "This explains so much..."

I gave a short, sharp laugh. "Her name was Isabella."

"Oh no. All this time..." His eyes widened, his jaw dropping. "No wonder you didn't want me to call you bella! I'm so sorry."

He turned my palm over, kissing it repeatedly.

"She was stillborn." It was so hard to talk about it, even now, but another part of me felt relieved to be sharing it—sharing her. "I was thirty-eight weeks pregnant. Almost full term."

"That's... tragic."

Tragico. The ultimate tragedy. Yes, tragic was the perfect word.

"Is this why you got divorced?"

I shrugged, looking away. "Maybe partly. It was hard."

"I can't imagine." He held me closer, cradling my head on his shoulder. "Poor bella..." He sighed, smacking himself in the forehead. "Stupid! I won't call you that anymore."

"No, it's okay," I assured him. "I actually like it."

"You do?"

I nodded. "I miss her, and you calling me bella... it reminds me. In a good way. I love hearing her name."

"Bella, bella, bella," he whispered, kissing my forehead. "You are so brave, so sweet."

I tilted my head up and pressed my lips to his, closing my eyes and losing myself in the kiss. It wasn't difficult to do. Being with Nico always transported me somewhere outside of myself and yet kept me firmly present in the world at the same time.

The kiss deepened and I slipped my hand behind his neck, our tongues meeting, doing an electric dance. Wanting him happened so fast, it always surprised me.

"The bedroom," I murmured.

There was more than just a bed in it now—a night table, a dresser. Nico sat on the bed as I closed the door. I went to him, so overwhelmed with my own confession I could barely stay on my feet. He pulled me into his arms, buoying me up.

"Are you all right?"

"Just dizzy I guess," I whispered, running my fingers through his dark, thick curls. "Too much emotion in the past few weeks."

"Poor bella." He kissed me softly, his hands moving over my back, petting me.

"I don't want to talk anymore," I pleaded. "Let's not talk."

"Yes." He kissed me more deeply, his tongue twining with mine, exploring the soft recesses of my mouth. I didn't want to talk or think. I just wanted to be with him, to be as close as I could get to him. I thought briefly about Mason, and felt a little guilty, but I knew he would be gone for hours.

"Undress for me." Nico leaned back on the bed and watched, expectant.

I slid my t-shirt off over my head, tossing it on the floor. My bra was front hook and that came off too. By the time I was unbuttoning my jeans, he was unbuttoning his own, freeing his cock. I bit my lip at the sight of it, at the casual way he stroked himself as I stripped for him.

When I was naked, I crawled up between his legs on the bed, nuzzling his hand out of the way and taking his cock in my mouth. He made a soft noise in his throat, watching me lick the head. I loved the way he curved under my tongue, the thick feel of it sliding into my mouth. He reached for my breast, letting it fill his hand, teasing my nipple as I sucked him.

"Touch yourself," he said.

I reached down to part my pussy lips, my fingers sliding in the wetness, finding my clit and rubbing. Nico's hands kneaded my breasts, thumbing my nipples, driving me to distraction. I couldn't concentrate on sucking him when he did that and I squirmed on the bed.

"Come here." He reached for me and I crawled my way up, peeling his shirt off as I went. It was his gondolier uniform, black and white stripes. I tossed it off the bed, letting him guide me further up, up, until I was straddling his chest. His eyes drank me in, his gaze moving over my breasts, down my belly, focusing on the parted, swollen lips of my pussy.

"So beautiful." He used one finger to trace the swell of my mound, teasing my clit briefly, watching my face. "Touch yourself, Dani. I want to watch you come."

"Like this?" I bit my lip, cupping my pussy, rocking my palm against my flesh. His eyes lit up when I parted my pussy lips, showing him more pink, giving him a glimpse of my hooded little clit. It was throbbing.

Nico slipped a hand down to grab his cock. I glanced back and saw him fisting the length, rubbing the tip with his thumb as he watched me. I held my pussy lips open with one hand so he could see, using the fingers of my other to rub myself, first my clit in little circles, then sliding down to my hole. So juicy, nice and wet. I rubbed the slickness into my clit.

"Faster," he insisted, licking his lips. "Finger yourself."

I slid two fingers into my pussy, using my thumb to strum against my clit, rocking on top of him. My breath came faster, my nipples hardening. I saw him looking from my breasts to my pussy to my face, like he couldn't decide where to focus. He stroked himself faster, matching my rhythm, his eyes half-closed.

"It feels so good," I whimpered, rubbing myself feverishly now. Nico fixated on my pussy, his eyes glazed, as I got closer and closer to orgasm. "Oh God. I'm gonna come. Yes! Oh now! Now!"

My body announced my climax, my hips bucking, pussy snapping closed on my plunging fingers. I cried out and arched my back, feeling dizzy and looking to steady myself. Nico's hands went to my hips, holding me up, supporting me as my orgasm rushed through me, a fire in my veins.

"Beautiful," he breathed, and I looked down, seeing how wet his chest was with my pussy juices. The hair there glistened with it.

"Oh my fucking God," I said in English, rolling onto the bed with a soft groan.

"I don't know about God." Nico smiled. "But you can fuck me."

I laughed, lifting my head to look at him, still so very hard, his cock dripping with precum.

"Do you want to fuck me?" I shifted on the bed, lifting my ass in the air. "Do you want to slide into my hot, wet, tight—?"

He groaned, shoving his pants and boxers down and rolling up next to me on the bed so fast I barely had time to register it. Then he was sliding his cock home, shoving my legs apart with his, driving me forward on the bed. I cried out as he thrust, deeper, harder, slamming the bed against the wall.

"Oh God!" I grabbed onto the edge of the mattress. "Oh God! Oh God!"

Nico leaned over me, still thrusting, his breath hot in my ear. "I love fucking you."

"Yes!" I agreed, giving back as good as I was getting, grinding and rolling my hips. "Yes! Yes, yes, yes!"

God help me, I loved getting fucked by him.

"That's it," he growled, driving me further up on the bed. "Take that cock. Take it!"

I took it. My pussy squealed and squelched in protest, the sound of our fucking filling the room, but I took him, his hands cupping my breasts, my nipples hard under his fingers as we bucked together on the bed. His teeth grazed my shoulder, his mouth sucking at the flesh of my neck as he pressed me down onto the bed, forcing me to take his full weight.

"Nico," I gasped, wiggling under him, his cock at an extreme angle, impaling me again and again. He forced my legs wide with his, hips making fast, hard circles, his pelvis rocking against my ass.

"Rub your pussy," he insisted, panting in my ear. "Get yourself off. I want to come inside you."

I twisted my hips so I could reach my pussy from underneath, rubbing furiously at my throbbing clit, closing my eyes and just letting him fuck me. The hard, thrusting swell of his cock drove me on, and I surrendered to the sensation, letting him take me just where I'd wanted to go all along. It was exquisite torture, our bodies shiny with sweat from the effort.

"Oh fuck!" He slowed, but I knew it was too late. I could feel how his cock swelled inside of me, beginning to pulse. "Ohhhhhh fuck! Fuck! I'm coming!"

"Yes!" I gasped and spread for him, arching my back and giving him more of my pussy, taking him as deep as I could. My own orgasm chased his, finally catching up just as the last of his cum overflowed my capacity, seeping out around the base of his cock. I screamed as the force of it surged through me, fully alive and electric, the thundering force of it threatening to melt me into a puddle on the mattress.

"Oh bella." He collapsed, kissing me deeply before rolling to the side, pulling me in close and yanking the covers over us. I didn't say anything, but snuggled back happily in his arms, too dazed and confused to do anything else. We rested like that for a long time, quiet, our breathing deep and even.

I thought about going home. I didn't want to be here when Mason got back. Nico was breathing deep and even beside me, and I thought he was asleep. He probably thought I was too.

Which is why I didn't say a word when he kissed my temple and whispered, "Choose me, bella. Choose me. Please, choose me."

I just kept my eyes closed.

Chapter Six

Dear Carrie and Doc,

I am so confused. I know you said I just need to be honest with them, and myself, and I know you're right. But what if I don't know what I want? If I don't know my own heart?

I'm sorry I keep laying things on you like this, but when I write to you, somehow things get clearer. I start figuring out what's going on in my head, and things inevitably come out that I didn't even realize I felt. I know you said you don't mind, but I feel like I have to apologize anyway. You've got enough going on with school and Janie and your own life. Like you need my problems too?

I'm trying to be honest and truthful about my feelings. I'm trying to figure out what it is I really want. A life with Mason? A life with Nico? The third option would be a life without either of them, which I can't even begin to conceive of. Losing them both would break my already-broken heart into another million little pieces, and I just don't think I could pick them all up this time.

Mason's been my best friend for years. We've been through so much together. Even after we divorced, I never stopped loving him. I think we both needed the time and space and distance to grow. To grow up. To heal too. We're so much better now than we ever were before.

But Nico... he's so sweet, so generous and open and tender. How can I not love him too? And it isn't just physical. If it were just the sex, I could give that up. We have so much in common—a love for this country, for the people and the food. We spend hours roaming galleries together, talking about art and culture. He's so passionate, about life, about everything. About me. He makes me feel alive in ways I haven't in so long.

The truth is, I'm selfish.

I want them both.

And I know, I know. It's just not possible...

"Easter means you can eat chocolate again?" I asked Nico, holding one of his sister's homemade truffles just out of his reach.

"Don't tease the animals, dear." Mason snatched the chocolate from my hand, tossing it to Nico, who caught it and stuffed it into his mouth before I could even protest.

"Meanie!" I stuck my tongue out at him. "You never let me have any fun."

"Are they good?" Giulia asked, shifting the baby over her shoulder. He was bigger now, a few months old, able to hold his own head up, gazing around at us with big, dark eyes. Just looking at him made my uterus hurt. Literally. The cramps came in waves, although my period wasn't due for another week.

"Fantastic, as always." Nico kissed his sister's cheek, leaving a smear of chocolate there. She laughed, wiping it off, as her brother reached for his nephew, lifting him high in his arms, making the baby giggle. When Luka's eyes got wide, being so high, Nico handed him back to his sister before the baby could begin to cry.

"You're such a tease." Mason sat next to me on the sofa, putting an arm casually around my shoulder. Nico saw this and sat on my other side, taking my hand. I couldn't help the heat filling my cheeks, seeing Mama Dorotea frowning in our direction, the way Nico's sister Anna and her husband glanced at us from where they were playing cards at the dining room table with the kids.

Caprice, being the precocious teenager she was, looked between the three of us with big eyes and started asking the questions everyone wanted to know—in English, of course, because Mason didn't speak much Italian. "So you're married?"

"We *were* married," I corrected her. "We're divorced now."

She wrinkled her nose, looking between Mason and her brother, the confusion apparent on her face. "But... what are you doing here then?"

"Visiting," Mason replied.

"So you're not together anymore," Caprice went on, pushing him to clarify.

"Hey, Anna, did you get your landlord to fix your leaky sink?" I inquired, trying to change the subject.

I could hear Mama Dorotea in the kitchen muttering something in Italian. She hadn't said much to the three of us, but I caught the word *"bastardo"* and winced, glad Mason didn't know the language. She was still angry that Nico had moved out. I was surprised she'd invited us to Easter at all, but then again, I'd overheard Nico saying, "If they can't come, I won't be coming either," so that might have had something to do with it.

"Of course not." She rolled her eyes, slapping a card down on the table. "Ha! I win the *re bello*!"

"What's that?" I asked, getting up off the sofa and going over to the table. It was a good excuse to get away from Caprice's questions.

"The beautiful king," Anna said in English, kissing the card and holding it up to Sal, who scowled in her direction. "It's *Scopa*. Do you want to play?"

"No thanks. I'll just watch." Although I knew the rules, I'd only played a few times. It was a lively game, and the family quickly slipped back into speaking Italian, laughing and slapping cards down on the table. Soon Mason and Nico had wandered over to the table to watch as well, but I was glad to see that Caprice had decided to stay with Giulia and Will in the living room so she could cuddle the baby.

I didn't like to get too close to the baby. When he'd been such a tiny newborn, with all that dark hair, he'd reminded me so much of Isabella it physically hurt me to look at him. Now it was better, although I swear my belly contracted every time I glanced over there, as if aching for a life of its own. I'd sworn, after she was born, that I would never have another. I said I'd never risk going through that again, whatever the chances might be.

Mason had been heartbroken. In spite of our young age, in spite of his parents' relief—yes, relief—at our daughter's death, in spite of our precarious financial situation, in spite of everything, he'd wanted to try again right away. It was one of the things that had driven us apart. Just thinking about having another baby brought a stab of fear and pain so great it made me feel faint.

"Are you okay?" Mason asked at my elbow.

I glanced back at him and smiled. "Fine."

"You look pale," Nico said. He was behind me, on my other side, watching the game. In the other room, the baby cried, and the pain in my middle increased as if in response. I gasped, my hand instinctively moving to cover my lower belly. The cramping, which had been dull and constant, suddenly became a sharp, stabbing thing.

"Are you sure you're okay?" Mason again.

I struggled for breath to speak. The pain had taken it. "I don't know."

"What is it?" Nico turned me to face him, frowning.

Everyone was looking now. Even Mama Dorotea, who had heard the concern in her son's voice, had appeared in the kitchen doorway, a turkey baster in her hand. In the next room, I heard the baby crying in earnest now. Probably hungry, I thought, remembering how my breasts had ached after Isabella was born, making milk for a baby who would never eat.

"I'm just a little dizzy," I managed to whisper, but the room was receding, going black at the edges, and I knew it was more than that. Something was suddenly very, very wrong.

The last thing I remembered was Mason and Nico kneeling over me, the sound of a baby crying far away, and me, speaking my daughter's name like a prayer.

"What happened?" I croaked, opening my eyes to the same sight—Mason on one side, Nico on the other. This time they each occupied a rail, leaning over to look at me in the hospital bed. I knew I must have fainted—I remembered that much. And the pain, the sharp, stabbing, searing pain in my belly. That was gone now.

"There's my bella." Nico smiled, brushing hair out of my face.

Mason, not to be outdone, leaned over and kissed my forehead. "Hey beautiful."

"What happened?" I asked again, swallowing hard. My throat hurt. Why did my throat hurt? "Can I have some water?"

They both reached for it at the same time, but the Styrofoam cup was on Mason's side. He held it for me while I sucked on the straw, peering at them over the lip of the cup.

"You're going to be all right," Nico soothed. He spoke softly in Italian, smoothing my hair, picking up where Mason had left off.

"English, please," Mason insisted, glaring at him as he put the water back on the table. "Dani, you had to have an operation."

"What?" I half sat, looking around the room. There was another bed, but no occupant. No nurse or doctor was in the room. "What kind of operation?"

"Your womb," Nico said, speaking English. "She was damaged."

I looked at Mason, wide-eyed, feeling my limbs turn to ice. "What is he talking about?"

"It was your IUD." Mason swallowed, glancing toward the door, probably hoping a nurse or someone else would come in and tell me the rest. Dear God, what was the rest? Did I want to know? I could already imagine. I'd gotten the intrauterine device right after we'd lost Isabella. Mason and I had fought long and hard about it. He didn't want to use any birth control—he desperately wanted another baby. I remembered telling him, "Babies aren't like light bulbs. You can't just go out and replace them." I'd won that argument.

"Wait..." I looked between them, up on my elbows, wearing just a hospital gown, a thin sheet as cover. I was afraid to look beneath it. I couldn't feel much of anything, but I was woozy. They'd probably pumped me full of pain meds. "No. Please tell me..." I swallowed, the thought so beyond comprehension I almost couldn't speak it. "Please tell me it's not gone. I'll... will I still be able to have children?"

Mason looked at me, surprised. "Do you want to?"

"I..." I blinked back tears. "I don't know. What difference does it make?"

Mason shrugged. "I just... I just remembered you saying, after Isabella..."

"Your IUD perforated the uterus," Nico interrupted. "You had internal bleeding."

"You lost a great deal of blood," Mason reiterated. "That's why you fainted."

"So did they take it?" My voice was choked, hoarse.

"No, no," Nico assured me, clasping my hand. Mason took the other one. "They stopped the bleeding and repaired it."

I sat back, shaking in relief, so surprised at my own reaction I could barely speak.

"How long do I have to stay here?" I glanced around at the white walls, the curtain half-pulled around the bed.

Mason looked at Nico. "The doctor said until tomorrow."

"But you can't go back to your place," Nico chimed in. I stared at him. "You can't be alone. You need someone to be with you for at least a week."

"So you're coming home with us."

"With you?"

Nico nodded, leaning over and kissing my cheek. "We'll take good care of you."

"My bedroom's near the bathroom," Mason said, unlocking the apartment door.

"Mine's by the kitchen," Nico countered.

"My bed's easier to get in and out of."

"Mine's bigger."

"Mine—"

"Oh for God's sake, I'll sleep on the couch!" I cried, plopping down on it and pulling a blanket over my head. "I'm glad the furniture finally arrived!"

"Now see what you did?" Mason sighed.

"Me?" Nico scoffed. "You started it."

"Are you two-year-olds?" I pulled the blanket down, rolling my eyes. "Keep it up and I'm going back to my place, no matter what the doctor said."

Jezebel came wandering out of the kitchen. She perked up upon seeing me, leaping onto the arm of the sofa beside me and swishing her tail. I petted her head and she purred.

"Thank you for taking care of her."

"Of course." Mason smiled. "And you don't have to sleep on the couch."

"Let's not start this again. The couch will be fine."

"Are you hungry?" Nico asked. "I made soup."

I smiled at him. "Starving."

We all sat on the couch and watched a marathon of *La Piovra*—Italy's version of *The Godfather* as a television series—and ate soup. Even Jezebel came to lick the remains out of my bowl. I found myself dozing off, leaning first on Mason's shoulder, then adjusting to lean against Nico's. Both men cradled me, petted me, rubbing my head or my feet.

"Sleepy bella." Nico kissed my cheek. "We should let her rest."

"That's probably a good idea."

"But it's early yet," I protested, glancing at the clock—only seven!

"Your body needs to heal," Mason insisted.

"And you do that best while you're sleeping."

I smiled. "Tag-teamed."

They glanced at each other, eyebrows raised.

"I didn't mean it that way." I flushed. "You're very, very bad men and I hate you both."

They kissed me goodnight, each of them. They both tasted like chicken noodle soup, but I savored the difference in the press of their mouths, the way Mason's lips parted a little, how Nico breathed me in with his kiss.

"Goodnight, Dani," Mason whispered.

"Goodnight, bella," Nico echoed.

I smiled, but I was so tired, I barely got the word out before I drifted off. "'Night."

The boat rocked back and forth and I clung to the sides, my knuckles white. The heat was close, blazing. My face was so hot it felt blistered. Ahead of me a hooded figure steered the gondola on a river of lava and I wondered if this was the River Styx. Was I dead? Was this death?

My first thought was Isabella. Would I see her again? What was past the barrier ahead?

A bony finger rose from the robe, pointing, and the boat came to a shaky stop. The river diverged into a V here, the rocky walls rising around us reflecting the orange heat of the lava below.

I had to choose.

I can't.

I shook my head, refused. The bony finger rose again. Choose.

No, no, no. Don't make me. Please don't make me choose. I begged.

The finger dropped and the figure was still. Relieved, I sat back in the boat, closing my eyes. It was out of my hands. Whichever way we went, I wasn't responsible.

The boat rocked hard and I jolted up. The gondola tilted so far to one side scalding lava began to seep over the edge. Then the other. The figure was going to tip the boat! I was going to be thrown in!

"No!" I cried, but the words were useless.

The boat flooded with fiery liquid and reached its tipping point, throwing me into a broiling hell of fire. I screamed, trying to swim in the searing heat, seeing the figure right the gondola, standing again at the edge and beginning to steer away.

I swam in the sweltering heat. Impossible. Why hadn't I melted into nothing? I was on fire, but the heat was white-hot, like needles, tiny knives, and I shivered in response. I was drowning in fire like ice, the pain making my whole body ache.

"Dani!"

I turned toward the sound of my name. Mason! Was he coming for me?

"Bella! Wake up!" Nico, calling me.

Choose. *The figure was back, standing over me, floating above the river of pain.* Choose.

"No!" I thrashed on the couch, feeling hands holding me down. "Cold," I muttered, shivering. I thought I'd kicked my blankets off, but no, there they were, tangled around my waist. Both men were standing over me in their boxer shorts. Had I called out?

Mason's hand on my forehead. "Oh Jesus Christ, she's burning up."

"Get her to the bed," Nico ordered.

"Whose?"

"I don't care!"

Mason carried me, the blankets dragging behind him. His bed was soft, the down comforter warm, but still I shivered. I couldn't stop.

"Keep me warm," I begged, reaching for Mason. He slid into bed beside me, glancing at Nico, and I called for him, too. "Please, Nico. Please." And he came as well, snuggled behind me, both of them putting their arms around me, a cocoon.

But even the heat from their bodies didn't help. Still, I shivered, my teeth chattering, even though they pulled the down-filled covers up to my chin, both of them smoothing my hair. I tried to sleep and I think I did, but I woke whimpering, feeling myself slipping into nothing, grasping for something to hold onto. Mason was there to hold me, Nico right behind.

"I'm so cold," I complained, burying my face in Mason's chest, feeling Nico's arms around me. I slept again, this time dreaming of hell, my own private version where Satan forced me into impossible choices over and over.

"What's wrong with me?" I woke up as Nico brought a thermometer, putting it under my tongue.

"Shhh." He soothed, looking over at Mason. "I think it's just a little bit of fever."

"Little my ass." Mason took the thermometer out as it beeped. "It's... forty? What the hell does that mean?"

Nico paled. "We need to call the doctor. That's about... a hundred and four degrees Fahrenheit."

"Hello, I need to speak to Dr. Selvaggi." Mason was on the phone before Nico even finished his sentence. "Dr. Selvaggi please," he repeated louder. "I need to speak to Dr. Selvaggi right now!"

Even I could hear the string of Italian coming from the receiver, which I knew was completely unintelligible to Mason.

Nico grabbed the phone, speaking fluent Italian. "Dr. Selvaggi's patient, Danielle Stuart, has a fever and I suspect she has an infection." He paused, listening. "Forty." He sighed in relief. "Thank you."

Mason re-appeared with a cool cloth, resting it on my forehead. It felt good, but I was still so cold! Nico talked to the doctor as Mason wiped my face and neck with the washcloth, whispering my name, kissing my cheek.

"What did he say?" Mason asked when Nico hung up the phone.

"He's going to prescribe antibiotics," Nico told him, switching back to English. "But he wants to see her on Monday."

I groaned. "No more doctors!"

"He also said we have to get her fever down."

Mason nodded. "Do you have aspirin?"

"Bring her into the bathroom." Nico was already heading out of the room.

"Can't you just go get it?" Mason called.

"We need to get her into the tub."

"What?" I protested, but Mason carried me and Nico ran the water. They undressed me like a child, fed me aspirins, and helped me to the tub.

I screamed, thrashing in the water, trying to escape. "It's freezing!"

"Keep her in." Nico's mouth was set in a grim line. "I have to get ice."

My teeth chattered so much, the noise in my head so loud, I could barely hear Mason's words as he grabbed my limbs, pushing me back in, something about holding still and being for my own good.

"Do we really have to do this?" Mason panted when Nico brought a bowl full of ice cubes into the bathroom.

"The doctor said to." Nico looked at me, his face pained. "If her fever gets much higher, she may start to have seizures. It could cause brain injury."

"Christ." Mason winced as Nico poured the ice in and I screamed again.

"Please," I begged them both, my eyes wild, so cold I couldn't feel my fingers where my nails dug into Mason's forearm. "Oh God, please, stop. Please!"

Nico's voice was hoarse. "I have to get more."

I sobbed, clinging to Mason, and then to Nico, when the freezer was empty of ice. They took turns soothing me, both men working to cool my feverish body as I writhed in the tub, begging for it to end.

Nico took my temperature, although I was shivering so much I could barely keep the thermometer between my chattering teeth.

"What is it?" Mason asked, his jaw tight.

Nico's shoulders visibly relaxed. "Better. Let's get her to bed."

A fluffy towel and four rough hands later, I was dry. One of Mason's t-shirts—it smelled comfortingly like him—went over my head and this time Nico carried me back to the bed.

"I'm so sorry," Nico whispered into my ear in Italian, kissing my cheek, my temple, as he pulled the covers up to my chin. "Hang on, bella. I love you."

"Just don't leave me." I put my arms around his neck and hung on.

The doorbell rang and Mason and Nico exchanged glances.

"It's the pharmacy," Nico said.

Mason was already heading toward the door.

And then there were more pills, two huge ones, big enough to gag a horse. I choked and spit water all down the front of me, wetting the t-shirt. Mason pulled it off and just covered me with the down-filled blanket again.

"Now what?" Mason sat next to me on the bed.

"We wait. We pray. We hope." Nico was on my other side, his cool hand pressed against my forehead.

Mason snorted. "Isn't there something a little more proactive we can do?"

"There's nothing but this." Nico spooned me, his arm around my waist.

"I'm still cold." I opened my eyes, seeing Mason looking at us, his expression unreadable. I reached for him, feeling desperate. "Please."

He came to bed, his breath warm on my cheek, his hand on my hip.

"Closer," I whispered, and he obliged. They both did, enveloping me, and I finally relaxed, this time falling into a dreamless, peaceful sleep with no fire, no ice.

Chapter Seven

Dear Carrie and Doc,

I need your advice. Nico and Mason are competing for me all the time. I think they've decided to live together—they're roommates now, at least for the time Mason is staying—just to drive me crazy. And to make sure they can both keep tabs on what I'm doing, of course. I feel so caught between the two of them and I don't know what to do.

Tell me. Please tell me what to do, who to choose. I'm at a loss. I don't trust my own compass or judgment, especially since it's telling me that I want them both. That can't be right. Something in me must be broken, off. I know this shouldn't be so hard, but every time I imagine leaving one of them for the other, I become paralyzed.

And it's not about hurting them, although I know I would hurt one if I chose the other. It's about me. I feel as if I'm connected to both of them in a very deep, profound way, and I'm not sure I am even capable of making such a difficult choice.

But I trust you both. I love you. And I know you want what's best for me. So I'm asking you, as your former lover and best friend, please, just tell me what to do. Whatever it is, I promise you, I swear to Nico's God and everything that is sacred in the world, that I will do it.

Just please, tell me which one to choose.

The doctor poked and prodded and confirmed that I had indeed developed an infection. The antibiotics were working, however—my fever was gone and I felt lighter already. There was no pain, and I'd inspected the incision sites. They'd done the surgery laproscopically, just four small cuts in my abdomen that were healing nicely. I'd have some scars on my belly to go with the stretch marks from Isabella, but considering that they'd saved my uterus, somehow I didn't mind so much.

The boys were in the lobby—I'd refused to let them follow me in, much to their chagrin. I took the opportunity to ask the doctor, "So about sex...?"

He raised his eyebrows and smiled. "Any time you're feeling up to it."

"Really?" I wasn't sure if I was hoping for a yes or a no, but leaving it up to me? That wasn't fair. I had enough choices to make, didn't I?

He assured me that it was perfectly safe, although I was glad Mason and Nico didn't hear him say so. He told me to continue to take it easy. I'd been anemic when I was admitted to the hospital, and although they were supplementing my iron and had given me a transfusion, he was concerned about fainting spells.

"I'm sure I'll be fine," I assured him, going out to find Nico and Mason talking in the lobby. They were laughing and the sight of something other than a scowl on either of their faces when they were together shocked me.

"Ready to go?" Nico looked up as I approached. I nodded, and Mason stood, taking my hand.

"I need a shower." Being submerged in ice was my last experience with bathing, and the memory wasn't a good one. I'd pretty much just slept in Mason's bed since, tucked between the two of them, trying to recover from my fever.

"We can do that," Nico piped up, taking my other hand.

I rolled my eyes. "I'm sure I can shower by myself."

"Actually, I'd like someone to supervise for a few days." The sound of the doctor's voice through the little lobby window startled me. He was handing a chart over to a nurse and had clearly overheard our conversation. He directed his words to Mason and Nico. "She may be unsteady on her feet for a while. Just keep an eye out."

Mason saluted. "Will do, Doc!"

The doctor saluted him back and Nico laughed. We took a water-bus back to their place, although I protested.

"I want my own bed, my own shower," I complained. "And Cara Lucia—"

"We've already told Cara Lucia all about it," Mason assured me.

"And I brought your books and I contacted your professors," Nico added.

I blinked at them. "Did you bring me underwear too?"

"Actually..." Nico and Mason looked at each other. "We did."

"Then I guess you've thought of everything." I grimaced, crossing my arms over my chest and watching the rain fall. I was glad we had the cover over us. It was really coming down. According to Nico, the weather had been beautiful while I was in the hospital, unseasonably warm, almost like summer, but spring had returned with a vengeance.

Mason and Nico talked over my head—something about a football game, which really meant soccer. I was surprised Mason was interested, given his usual disdain for most sports, but from the gist of the conversation, they'd apparently watched an exciting game together while I was in surgery, and now Mason was hooked.

"I'm going to have to go back to my flat eventually," I argued as we got off the bus.

It was only a few blocks to their place, but by the time we reached it, I was really starting to feel tired. Maybe I had overdone it a little bit on my first venture out.

"You put her to bed," Nico said to Mason as soon as we got up the stairs. "I'll make her some lunch."

"But I need a shower!" I protested, nearly tripping over Jezebel, who wound herself around my feet and mewed plaintively.

"Okay, shower first." Mason nudged Jezebel out of the way but they all followed me to the bathroom. I stood in the doorway while Nico started the water and Mason got a towel out of the closet.

"Thanks, you guys." I waved them out. "I can handle it from here."

They exchanged looks, some sort of communication passing between them.

"I don't think so." Mason shut the door, leaning against it and looking at me. It locked behind him.

"Remember what the doctor said?" Nico reminded me.

Mason had my shirt peeled off before I knew what was happening. Nico worked the button and zipper on my jeans, wedging them down my hips. I protested, but then my bra and panties were gone too, and they were putting me in the shower.

"I really don't need two babysitters." I sighed, reaching for the soap. I could smell myself, rank and strong. How could they even stand to be in the same room with me?

"Are you doing all right?" Nico called.

I rolled my eyes, turning around and tilting my head back so the water could wet my hair. That's when I nearly passed out. The whole bathtub moved, or at least I felt like it did, and I stumbled, my palms slipping on the slick tile, trying to hold onto something to keep from falling. I think I cried out, I'm not sure, but Mason was in the shower with me in an instant, still in jeans and a t-shirt, holding me up.

"What happened?" I whispered, clinging to him.

"You lost a lot of blood," Nico reminded me. Not to be outdone, he'd stepped into the shower to rescue me too, still in his clothes as well.

I looked between them and laughed. "This is ridiculous."

"You're right." Mason grinned, pulling off his t-shirt and tossing it outside the curtain. Nico followed suit, and before I knew it, they both had their jeans and boxers off too, and we were all standing there naked in the shower together.

"You two are crazy." I shook my head, still laughing, but I was overwhelmed with gratitude when they both grabbed a washcloth and some soap and started washing—not themselves, but me.

"I still feel really weak," I admitted. It was strange to have them touching me like this, together, but familiar too.

"Let us do all the work." Nico soaped my hair and Mason helped him rinse it, both men massaging my scalp, making me tingle.

Then they turned their attention to my body, Nico's big hands moving down over my back and shoulders. I giggled when he made me lift my arms so he could scrub under them from behind.

"It's a hard job, but somebody's got to do it." Mason grinned, giving up the washcloth and using his hands to soap my breasts and belly. "Sorry, buddy," he said to Nico, looking at him over my shoulder. "I got all the fun parts." Mason's hand moved down between my legs, soaping me there, too. I gasped.

"Not all of them." Nico was close behind me and I felt his hand slip down the crack of my ass.

"You're bad," I whispered, biting my lip when Nico's soapy fingers probed gently at my asshole, Mason still cupping my mound. "Oh God."

"Let us take care of everything," Mason murmured, his fingers slippery against my pussy. I buried my face in his shoulder, my arms around his neck, the warm water falling all around us, creating a cloud of steam. I felt even weaker in the shower than I had on our outing and I let them both hold me up, pressed between their flesh.

"It feels so good," I murmured against Mason's neck, arching, feeling Nico's hand probing my pussy too from behind, Mason's from the front, both of them seeking my heat.

"Sweet bella." Nico kissed my wet head and I felt his cock against my ass, incredibly hard. Mason was hard too, rising up toward my navel. How could I have expected anything less? And still, it surprised me to be sandwiched between them like this, their kisses gentle on my shoulders, my cheeks, both of them saying my name.

"I love you, Mason," I whispered, pressing myself more fully into the circle of his arms. I glanced over my shoulder as Nico wrapped his arms around my waist, nibbling my shoulder. "I love you, Nico."

God help me. I did. I loved them both.

"I'm feeling dizzy," I said, my breath coming far too fast. They both rinsed me off and helped me out of the shower, drying me first and wrapping me up in a towel, and then themselves. They led me back to Mason's room, to the bed. He'd changed the sheets from when I was so sick, so they were clean and fresh.

"There you are." Nico tucked me in, a towel still wrapped around his waist. Mason was pulling on a pair of boxers.

"Don't go." I grabbed his hand, pulling him toward me.

"I have to make lunch," Nico said, but he slid under the covers beside me anyway, taking me into his arms.

"Mason," I called, reaching for him too. He pulled the covers aside and spooned me from behind. I smiled, pressed between them. "I like this."

That was an understatement. When we'd first been like this, I was sick, practically delirious. Now, although I was still a little weak, I was far more aware of the feel of their bodies against mine, the long press of Nico's thigh, the grip Mason had on my hip. Neither of them could seem to keep their hands off me, roaming over my bare skin under the sheet, exploring hills and valleys.

I arched back against Mason, wiggling my behind into the saddle of his hips, feeling the hard length of his cock tenting his boxers. He made a small noise in his throat, his fingers digging into my hip.

"I got you both all excited," I whispered, watching Nico's eyes darken when I reached under his towel. He was hard too, pulsing in my hand.

"You did," Nico agreed, biting his lip, eyes half-closing in pleasure as I began to stroke him.

"Can you blame us?" Mason kissed my shoulder, my neck, his cock wedging itself further against the crack of my behind.

"You really should rest, bella. You're still not well." Nico moaned when I thumbed the head of his cock, rubbing at the frenulum, so sensitive.

I stuck my tongue out at him. "The doctor said I could."

"He did?" I heard the hopeful tone in Mason's voice and chuckled, rolling onto my back and reaching for his cock too.

"You should still take it easy," Nico warned, but his cock was swelling in my fist.

"This *is* easy," I murmured, drawing them both closer by tugging on their cocks. Nico had lost his towel and Mason's boxers were pulled down, the elastic caught under his balls. I pushed the covers away so I could see, working each cock in my fist, stroking them into the crook of my thighs.

"Oh God." Mason groaned, cupping my breast, the one closest to him. Nico did one better, lowering his head to suck my nipple between his lips, making me whimper and squirm between them.

"You've got such beautiful breasts," Nico whispered. My flesh filled their hands, both of them thrusting against me.

"Doesn't she?" Mason joined him in sucking my tits, their tongues making hot, wet trails. "Oh fuck, Dani, you jerk me off so good."

Nico moaned against my breast, his hand finding its way down between my legs. I was still a little moist from the shower, but I was more wet from having their hard cocks in my hands, knowing how much they both wanted me. His finger moved down my slit, opening me, finding my hole.

"Is that a good idea?" Mason frowned, watching Nico's fingers move in and out of me.

I moaned, rocking up against his hand. "I'd say it's a very good idea."

"Are you sure?" Mason reached down, parting me with his fingers, giving Nico more room to fuck me with his.

"Rub my clit," I whispered to Mason, shifting my hips up. He strummed it gently, making me shiver, his cock getting bigger in my hand. They were both breathing hard, playing with my pussy and letting me stroke them, all of us finding an easy rhythm.

"Who's gonna come first?" I teased, thumbing the head of Mason's cock and squeezing Nico's tight in my fist. They both groaned against my breasts.

"You are," Mason panted, making fast circles over my throbbing clit. Nico redoubled his efforts too, plunging his fingers into my pussy.

"Nuh-uh." I gasped, jerking them faster, pointing them toward my pussy where their hands were busy trying to get me off. And they were going to succeed, sooner rather than later. Nico's fingers squelched in my pussy, fucking me hard, and Mason was incredibly skilled, knowing just where to touch me, pushing me closer and closer to climax.

"Oh God." I groaned, thrashing on the bed. Their tongues made hot circles against my nipples and they glistened like dark jewels in the lamp light. "Oh yes! Yes!"

I bucked my hips up, sure that Mason had been right—I was going to come first. His cock was stiff,

Nico's too, both of them like steel thrusting in my hands.

"That's it, baby," Mason urged, looking at my face, my eyes half-closed with pleasure. "Come for me."

"Come for *me,*" Nico insisted on my other side, and I could have sworn there were a thousand fingers working between my legs, sending white-hot sparks through my limbs.

Mason met Nico's eyes and grinned, moving his fingers down to join Nico's, his thumb staying on my clit. They were both fucking me now, their fingers stretching me wide.

"Come for us," Mason panted, thrusting hard into my fist, aiming toward my aching pussy. "Come on, baby, come for us!"

"Yes, bella," Nico urged. "Come for us. Come all over our hands."

I glanced between them and groaned, unable to hold out any longer. My pussy was on fire, the wet sound of them finger-fucking me filling the room.

"I'm gonna come," I whispered, glancing down to see them working my pussy over, their cocks like arrows pointing the way. "Oh yes! Yes! Make me come!"

"Oh fuck!" Mason groaned and shoved his hips against me, his cock spewing cum all over my pussy, their fingers plunging hard and fast. "Oh my fucking God!"

Nico moaned on the other side of me, his dick swelling in my hand and then bursting, showering my pussy with cum, shooting it so far it left ropy strings all over Mason's cock and balls. I cried out, shuddering with astonished delight, my pussy clamping down on their fingers, a delicious flutter that spread outward from my pelvis in pulsing waves.

"What a mess," I gasped, laughing, looking down between my legs.

"I have just the thing." Nico, still out of breath, wiped his hand and cock off with the towel he'd brought to bed, handing it to me. I cleaned myself up too.

"Were you a boy scout?" Mason asked, taking the towel and rubbing his crotch clean.

Nico cocked his head. "What's a boy scout?"

I laughed, snuggling up to him. "Boy scouts must not be big in Italy."

"What's a boy scout?" Nico asked again, looking over my head at Mason as he spooned me from behind.

"Never mind." Mason smiled, kissing the top of my head. "Let's just get our girl down for a nap."

I raised an eyebrow at him. "I'm not a baby."

"You're my baby." He kissed me softly and pulled the covers up over all of us.

I closed my eyes and drifted, safe and warm in their arms.

⟡⟡⟡

When I woke up, I was alone, and the bed felt empty, cold, even with Jezebel curled up at my feet. I could hear them talking, the television on. I put on one of Mason's button down shirts, buttoning it as I opened the bedroom door. They were talking in the living room. How long had I slept?

"Hey, there she is." Mason smiled as I came into the room, patting the sofa. Nico was on the other side of it and there was a football game on the television. "How'd you sleep?"

"I feel like I've been sleeping for days." I slipped in between them on the couch.

"You have." Nico smiled. "Now that you're awake, I'll get dinner started."

I raised my eyebrows. "I missed lunch?"

"Afraid so," Mason replied. "Some amazing pasta thing. There's leftovers in the fridge though. If I don't stop eating this many carbs, I'm gonna gain fifty pounds."

"You get used to it." I laughed. "And you'll get addicted to Nico's cooking."

"Speaking of cooking, I've got to run to the market." Nico stood, leaning over to kiss the top of my head. He glanced at Mason. "Take care of her while I'm gone."

"Always." Mason's arm went around my shoulder, pulling me closer.

"What are you making us?" I snuggled up to Mason, watching Nico put on his jacket and shoes.

"It's a surprise." He smiled. "Be right back."

"Do I have any real clothes?" I asked Mason, feeling his hand moving in my hair, stroking gently. "I can't go around wearing your shirts all day."

"I don't see why not." His hand moved over my shoulder, massaging. "You're quite fetching in them."

I stuck out my tongue at him. "Fetch me some clothes."

They'd raided my flat, bringing jeans and t-shirts and sweaters. Panties and bras too. Mason had cleared out one of his drawers for me, and just seeing our clothes together in the same dresser again made my heart almost stop. That, more than anything else, gave me pause. Were we really doing this again?

I felt much better in my own clothes, joining Mason in the kitchen where he was cutting up an orange and boiling water for tea.

"Vitamin C," he said, putting the orange in front of me with a napkin. "Nico says it will help you heal."

"He's a pretty amazing guy, isn't he?" I mused, biting into the sweet, fleshy part of the orange.

"I guess he kinda is." Mason sat at the table with me. "But you picked him, so I guess I shouldn't expect anything less."

I smiled, watching him get up and pour water, dunking in a tea bag, thinking about this morning. Had it really happened, or was I dreaming?

"You really scared us, you know." Mason set the tea in front of me along with some sugar and milk. "I was afraid we might actually lose you."

We? I thought it, but didn't say it.

"I'm glad we didn't." He didn't meet my gaze but I thought I saw a tell-tale shine in his eyes. "I couldn't lose you too. Not after losing her."

"You did lose me once." I stirred my tea, thoughtful.

"Not like that." He blinked fast. "Not forever."

"Yeah." I sighed.

"With you, at least I knew I had a chance." His hand found mine under the table, squeezing. "With Isabella, there was no going back. She was just...gone."

Now I was the one blinking back tears. "I wish she wasn't."

"Me too."

"But we could have another baby."

He looked at me, surprised. "We could?"

"The doctor said we could," I reminded him.

"You know I'd like that." Mason smiled. "But what about you?"

I smiled back. "I think I'd like that too."

I thought for sure I saw tears in his eyes now, and he stood, heading toward the living room. "Drink your tea. Want to come watch football with me?"

"Soccer, you mean?" I asked, joining him on the sofa.

He scoffed. "It's called football here in Italy."

"You'll be assimilated yet," I said with a laugh.

"Well on my way, apparently."

We snuggled on the couch until Nico came in, arms loaded with groceries. I got up to help, but both men refused to let me. They tucked a blanket around my legs on the sofa and forced me to drink more tea while they worked in the kitchen. Mason acted as sous chef and I listened with great amusement as he followed all of Nico's orders.

"It is ready yet?" I called, taking a break from reading. "I'm starving!"

"Pazienza!" Nico snapped. "Patience, patience!"

But he brought me an antipasti, the appetizer, *polop pane e olive*—olives and octopus on bread. It was so good it only made my stomach rumble more loudly.

"Oh my God, what is that?" I heard Mason exclaim from the kitchen. When Nico responded, Mason stuck his head out to say, "I've never had octopus before."

I laughed. "What do you think?"

"It's amazing!"

That was just the beginning of amazing. The salad was made with wild greens and dressed with balsamic and virgin olive oil. Even Mason ate it, and he rarely ate anything green. Nico made veal scallopini so tender it melted in our mouths. We moaned so often during dinner than anyone listening would have thought we were having sex!

And of course, we drank wine. It was more homemade wine, this bottle from Nico's sister, Anna, sweet and fruity and delicious.

"I have never had a meal this good," Mason said, leaning back in his chair with a satisfied smile. Nico was flushed with pride and he gulped down more wine.

"Even at *Il Ridotto?*" I asked. Mason had taken me there, as promised, and the food had been just as good as the first time—although I had to admit, there was something about Nico's cooking that set it apart somehow.

"Even there," Mason countered, shaking his head. "Nico, dude, you need to open a restaurant. You are totally missing your calling."

Nico shrugged, replying in English. "That requires capital I don't have, I'm afraid. I've been saving, but my mother was hoping I'd spend that on a wedding."

He looked at me and now I was the one flushing and gulping my wine.

"Listen." Mason leaned forward, serious. "Trust me when I tell you, a man should never do what his mother wants him to do—especially just because she wants him to do it."

I raised my eyebrows at him, but I didn't say anything.

"You have to do what *you* want," Mason urged. "Not what everyone else wants you to do."

Nico nodded, looking thoughtful. "Maybe you're right."

I wanted to ask Mason who he was and what he'd done with my husband—*ex-husband*. But looking at Nico, I also felt like jumping up and down for joy, because Mason was right. Nico was wasting himself and his talents.

We helped Nico clean up and ate dessert—a delectable version of tiramisu that was like a food orgasm in my mouth with every bite. Both men watched me eat it with longing in their eyes. We talked for a while about food and recipes. Then Nico and Mason got into a discussion about U.S. politics and I zoned out, wandering to the living room and resuming my reading for school.

But I was still recovering, apparently, because my eyes grew tired fast and I fell asleep on the couch. When both men tried to cover me with a blanket at bedtime, I protested, reaching for them.

"Put me to bed," I insisted.

They looked at each other, both asking, "Where?" at the same time.

Instead of responding, I showed them, taking off all my clothes and crawling into the middle of Mason's bed. He joined me on one side, with Nico on the other, and this time, we all just slept, back to belly, me tucked safely and happily right where I wanted to be— between them both.

Chapter Eight

Dear Carrie and Doc,

I understand your reluctance to make a choice. You can only imagine my own! I think Mason wants to marry me again. And Nico... he's clearly committed to a life with me, and I have a feeling he'd propose in a heartbeat if I gave him a hint of encouragement. What am I supposed to do? Things are getting more and more complicated by the day and I have to find a way out of this mess.

Complicated doesn't even begin to cover it, to tell you the truth. I have to tell you something, and I'm almost ashamed to admit it, even to both of you, with our history together. Mason and Nico and I... we've been together. The three of us. It started quite innocently, actually. I was ill (it's a long story, but I had a problem with my IUD. It's all fixed now and I'm better, but it was scary for a while there...) and Mason and Nico were just trying to help. I was feverish and feeling cold, and they both got into bed with me to keep me warm. Then, of course, I needed help in the shower...

Well, you can see where this is going, can't you?

So yes, we've all been together. Granted, the men don't seem to want to have anything to do with each other, per se. It's all about me. But their competition seems to have lessened since, and we all seem to get along better. Cooperate more, I guess you'd say. It's become like a little family of three. Like I used to be with you.

But I know, even if this has become a temporary solution, this isn't a real answer. Ultimately, I'm going

*to be forced to choose. And then what? How do I break
either man's heart?*

And my own in the process?

*I wish someone would tell me what to do. Won't
you please, please reconsider and point me down the
right path? I'm desperate. I trust you both so much. I
will truly follow your advice, whatever it is...*

"But we agreed!" Mason's voice rose even louder.
I'd been trying to study for a test I had tomorrow—I'd
gone to school for the first time that day, although I
hadn't moved back to my flat. Mason and Nico
wouldn't allow it, insisting I stay with them for a
while, "just in case."

I glanced up from my book, frowning at the look on
Mason's face. I knew it well. He could get explosively
angry very quickly. Even Nico poked his head out of
his room, frowning.

"Look, I came over here to do a job, and I'm going
to do it." Mason was trying to keep his anger in check,
sensing my unease, I could tell. "No, I don't want to
talk to mother. No. No!"

Mason rolled his eyes to the ceiling, shaking the
phone at it, and then put it back to his ear. "Hello,
Mother."

Well, this wasn't going to be good, I thought.

"I'm old enough to make that decision for myself,
but thanks for the input." Mason sat on one of the
overstuffed chairs, already looking defeated. "None of
your business... I told you, it's none of your business."

Nico wandered out, sitting next to me on the sofa.
Now Mason had an audience of two.

"Are you kidding me?" Mason gaped at the phone.
"So this was all your idea? Do you think I'm going to

just come running home to Mommy because you told Dad to pull the rug out from under me?"

Nico and I exchanged wide-eyed glances. I could see Mason's knuckles turning white from clutching the phone.

"Fine," Mason said through gritted. "I said fine! Fine!"

He hung up. "Stupid cunt."

"What was that about?" I asked in the smallest voice possible.

Mason stood, starting to pace. "My father, clearly under my mother's influence, has decided that taking our franchise overseas isn't a good idea."

Nico squeezed my hand and I looked over at him.

"What are you going to do?" Nico asked.

"I guess I'm going to pack." Mason turned and stalked off to his room.

Nico and I followed without a word, me leading the way.

"You're leaving?" I asked from the doorway. "Are you kidding me?"

"What else am I supposed to do?" Mason sat on the bed, head in his hands. "I can't fight them. She wins."

Nico stepped into the room beside me. "Aren't you the one who told me not to let anyone tell you what to do?"

"Smart ass." Mason barked a laugh, looking up at him."You should be glad I'm leaving, right? Isn't that what you want?" He waved his hand at me, scowling. "You can have Dani all to yourself again."

I went over to the bed, sitting beside him and taking his hand. "Mason, don't leave."

"Why?"

"Because I want you," I said, putting my head on his shoulder. "Here. With me. I love you."

Nico sat on his other side. "You have to stand up for yourself."

"Look who's talking," Mason snorted. We were all quiet and then Mason said, "Fuck. I'm sorry. I didn't mean that."

"Yeah, you did." Nico shrugged. "And you're right."

"I don't have anything here," Mason said. "No job. Nothing."

"You have me." I squeezed his hand, glancing over at Nico. "You have us."

Mason groaned, flopping back on the bed, throwing his arm over his eyes.

I snorted. "Well you don't have to sound so enthusiastic about it."

"It's not that." He uncovered his eyes, looking up at me. I smiled, leaning over and kissing his cheek.

"It'll be okay." I kissed the corner of his mouth. He hadn't shaved yet and his face was scruffy. He turned his head toward me, kissing me fully, sliding his hand behind my neck to draw me in deeper.

"I guess I could stay," he murmured. "I'm sure I could find something to do around here."

I slid my hand down his belly, searching for the button on his jeans. "I promise I'll keep you busy."

"Bad girl." Mason looked up at Nico, who was watching us with great interest, a hungry longing in his eyes. "You know, buddy, she may need two men around just to keep her out of trouble."

Nico gave him a lopsided smile, reaching over to cup my breast through my t-shirt. "You may be right."

"How should I distract you?" I grinned, standing up and pulling my shirt off over my head.

Mason's eyes lit up. "That's a good start."

"How about this?" I undid the front hook of my bra, letting my breasts spill free.

Nico made a soft noise in his throat, his hand going to his crotch. The growing bulge in his jeans made my mouth water. Mason had a matching one, his hand rubbing between his legs as he watched me unbutton and unzip my jeans, turning around so I could slide them down my hips. My panties came with them, exposing me completely to them both.

"Jesus," Mason whispered, sliding a hand down the front of his jeans as I stayed bent over like that, spreading my legs and showing them my pussy.

Nico had his jeans undone, his cock out already, his dark eyes glued between my legs. I rubbed myself for them, slow at first, teasing my flesh, then sliding two fingers inside. I heard Nico gasp when I did that. I was watching them both upside down, my hair dragging on the floor, all the blood rushing to my head.

"Come here." Mason grabbed my hips and I saw his cock was free now too. His aim was perfect—he impaled me in one hard thrust. I cried out, feeling my flesh give in to him. He guided my hips, nice and easy, and I glanced over my shoulder to see his eyes half-closed, watching where his dick disappeared between my legs.

"Gimme." I reached back, searching blindly for Nico's cock, and found it. He gave a low moan, thrusting into my hand. "Let me suck it."

Nico got up, standing beside us on the bed, giving me just what I wanted. His cock curved nicely down my throat and I sucked him deeply as Mason fucked me, his hips pounding me upward with every thrust, jolting Nico's dick further down my throat. They both groaned and grunted, but I couldn't say a word—my mouth was far too full. My pussy, however, was speaking for me, soaking wet and squelching, my juices running down Mason's cock, coating his balls with a sticky sheen.

"Oh God." Mason thrust deep and held me there. I felt his thighs quivering, the muscles taut, and knew he must be fighting his climax. "Easy. Easy."

"Here." I slid slowly out of him, making him groan, and turned around to face him. He helped me straddle him and I slid slowly down again, taking his entire length. "Better?"

Mason grabbed my hips, shaking his head. "It's all too good."

"We should take turns then." Nico smiled, following my mouth, kneeling up on the bed.

"Good idea." Mason watched me lean in to suck Nico's cock, the look in his eyes full of lust. I took my time, teasing the head with my tongue, licking the first glisten of precum off the tip. Mason wasn't fucking me hardly at all, his cock swollen and hard inside of me, just pulsing between my thighs.

"Such a good little cock whore." Mason praised me, pushing my hair away from my face so he could get a better look.

Nico groaned in agreement. "Suck it, bella. Oh yeah, you suck me so good!"

"That's fucking hot." Mason gasped. He couldn't take his eyes off the sight of me taking Nico's cock, watching his hips buck, shoving it as far into my throat as he could. I gagged, choking on it, my eyes watering.

Mason chuckled. "Here." He reached out, wrapping his hand around the base of Nico's dick, feeding it to me. "Does that help?"

"Mmmm," I agreed, taking Nico's length down to Mason's pumping fist. When I glanced up, I saw Nico looking at Mason, their eyes locked. Something was happening, some communication was passing between them that I wasn't a part of.

Nico reached down and tweaked Mason's nipple, making him gasp, his hips bucking up, shoving his cock deep inside of me. Encouraged by Mason's response, Nico gently twisted the other one, and Mason groaned, his cock moving, fucking me again. Mason's hand seemed to move all on its own, stroking Nico into my mouth. I was mesmerized by the sight, taking as much of his length as I could, my lips meeting Mason's hand with every pass.

"I want to taste you, bella." Nico slid his cock out of my mouth and but Mason didn't let go as I sat up on his cock, Nico leaning over Mason to reach my pussy. I moaned when his tongue probed my cleft, finding the aching bud of my clit. I stared in amazement, seeing Mason still jerking Nico's hard cock as he leaned in to lick my pussy, his tongue traveling down to where Mason was still fucking me.

"You taste so good," Nico panted, his hips rocking, his cock thrusting in Mason's fist. I shifted my hips back, giving him better access, his tongue probing and lapping my flesh, licking not just my pussy but the base of Mason's cock too.

"Wanna taste more?" I came up slowly, sliding Mason out of me, his cock thick with my juices. Nico's eyes met mine and I knew he was thinking the same thing I was. I fed it to him, rubbing Mason's cock over his lips and eager tongue, letting him take it into his mouth.

"Oh fuck." Mason groaned, Nico's dick practically purple in his fist, stroking him faster and pumping his hips up into Nico's mouth. "Oh my fucking God."

"Now that's hot," I whispered, my hand in Nico's hair, pressing his head down, making him gag a little on Mason length. "Who's the good little cock whore now?"

Mason chuckled, looking up at me. "Come here, you slut. I want to taste that pussy too."

I couldn't say no to that. I went to straddle his face, turning so I could watch Nico sucking Mason—and so I could play with Nico's cock too, rubbing the head with my palm as Mason jerked him. I rocked my hips and Mason made his tongue hard, letting me rub my slit over it, moaning and making circles at my clit.

Mason's hand slowed on Nico's cock, too distracted by the way my hips were grinding against his face, so I leaned over to take that sweet, curved length into my mouth. Now we made the perfect pleasure triangle, the soft sounds of our licking and sucking and muffled moans filling the room.

"Okay okay okay," Mason moaned, pushing me off him and taking his cock out of Nico's mouth. "You are too fucking good at that."

Nico wiped his mouth with the back of his hand and grinned. "My turn now?"

Mason's eyes widened. "I've never sucked a cock in my life."

"There's always a first time," I panted, rubbing my clit as I looked between the two of them.

Nico laughed. "I meant, my turn to fuck our bella."

"Absolutely." Mason pushed me fully to my back on the bed, spreading my legs and with his palms and then my pussy lips with his fingers.

"Put him in me," I begged, looking from him toMason. "Please!"

Nico positioned himself between my legs and Mason grabbed his cock, stroking it, still wet from my saliva, against my clit. "You want that hard cock, baby? You want that inside of you?"

"Yes!" I cried, lifting my hips in response, looking down at Nico's slick, curved length, Mason's hand able to grab so much more of it than I was. "Oh God, yes!"

"Here it comes, baby." Mason positioned him perfectly, the mushroom head teasing my hole. I glanced up at Nico, seeing him looking between my legs too, watching as Mason slid his cock into my pussy.

"Oh God!" I moaned, wrapping my legs around Nico's hips. "Oh that's so good!"

Steel heat and fire between my thighs. I wanted more.

"Kiss me." I pulled Nico in and his mouth met mine. I could taste Mason's cock on his tongue and I moaned, panting with lust. Turning my head, I saw Mason fisting his dick, watching us.

"Fuck her," he instructed, but Nico was already thrusting, his cock driving me against the bed.

I wrapped my arms around his neck, my legs around his waist, feeling the glorious length of his cock impaling me again and again. Nico whispered into my ear in Italian, telling me how beautiful I was, how sexy, how good I felt. I knew Mason couldn't understand him, but it didn't matter, I was pretty sure he couldn't hear him anyway.

"Don't stop," I whispered, my pussy twitching around his dick. "Oh God. Nico, please. Make me come! Please!"

"Mmmm." Mason rolled closer, his face near mine. "Look at me, Dani."

I did as he asked, Nico's cock pounding into me, my whole body stretched taut like wire.

"I want to see you come," Mason whispered, kissing my cheek, licking at the corner of my mouth, rubbing his scruffy chin over the soft, sensitive skin of my neck. "Come all over his hard cock, baby. Do it! Do it!"

I cried out, my nails digging into the hard muscles of Nico's biceps as he held himself over me, slamming my pussy with his cock, taking me right over the edge. My eyes never left Mason's face as I came, my climax wrenched from me, wracking my whole body with tremors. And then both men were kissing me, my face and shoulders and neck and breasts, showering me with sweetness.

"My turn." Mason grinned, getting up on his knees, and I moaned as they both rolled me onto my belly. Mason grabbed my hips and pulled me to my knees, taking me from behind. He didn't mess around, plunging his cock in deep, filling the space that Nico had just vacated.

"Suck me, bella." Nico was on the bed in front of me, offering his cock, and I took it like a baby looking to suckle. I wanted to be filled completely.

"Oh God she's got such a sweet little cunt," Mason groaned, reaching under me so he could grab onto one of my swaying breasts.

"And a hot little mouth," Nico moaned, grabbing a fist full of my hair. He moaned when I took the time to run my tongue around the head of his cock, tickling the ridge, teasing him.

"Ohhh!" I squealed when Mason grabbed both of my hips, slamming into me, shaking the whole bed, rocking it against the wall.

"That's it!" Nico's eyes lit up, watching Mason fuck me. "Do it hard!"

"Don't forget about his cock," Mason reminded me, slapping my ass for good measure.

I yelped, taking Nico between my lips again, the sensation of a cock in my mouth and my pussy at once almost too much for me to bear. I panted around his length, moaning as Mason's balls slammed wetly against my clit.

"Suck that cock!" Mason instructed, shoving me down on it with just the motion of his hips, driving his cock into me at the same time. "Oh fuck. Your pussy feels so good, baby. Ahhhh!"

"You want to swallow my cum?" Nico panted, his hips bucking up, the head of his dick choking me. "Ohhhh yes yes, I'm gonna come in your mouth!"

I just gagged and nodded and tried to suck him faster, feeling his balls tighten in my hand. Mason groaned behind me and I knew he was watching, his cock pistoning in and out of me at a furious pace.

"Do it!" he gasped, fucking me so hard it hurt, his fingers rubbing my clit. "Oh fuck! I'm gonna fill that hot little pussy with my cum! Are you ready for it, baby?"

I couldn't respond, Nico already flooding my mouth with a geyser of cum. My own climax surprised me, coming out of nowhere, my pussy convulsing around the length of Mason's cock again and again. He cried out at the sensation, plunging violently into me, like a jolt of lightning striking all of us, followed by the shaking of thunder as we all collapsed onto the bed in a sweaty, panting heap.

"Oh my God," I finally gasped, lifting my head and clearing my tangled hair out of my vision. "What was that?"

"Fucking fantastic," Mason muttered, his arm thrown over his eyes.

I sat up on my elbow. "I had no idea you were bi."

Mason snorted laughter. "News to me too."

"Nico?" I touched his thigh and he jumped, opening one eye to look at me. "You okay?"

"Dehydrated." He swallowed, closing his eyes again. "Need... water..."

I smiled. "Want me to get you a glass?"

He groaned and sat, shaking his head. "I have to pee anyway."

Leaning over, he kissed me softly before padding naked out the door, shutting it behind him.

"Wow." Mason let out a pent-up breath. "I mean... wow."

"Yeah." I stared up at the ceiling, lost in thought. I hadn't had an experience like that since...

"I have something to tell you." I sat up and turned to Mason, taking the opportunity while Nico was out of the room. "Remember the Baumgartners?"

Mason nodded. "Yeah."

"Well..." I confessed. "It wasn't exactly a platonic relationship."

He sat up on his elbow, frowning. "What do you mean?"

"We were sleeping together."

"All three of you?" he exclaimed.

I nodded. "It started out just with Carrie. But eventually things progressed, and I was sleeping with them both. And then... I sort of fell in love with them."

He cleared his throat. "Both of them?"

"I know it sounds impossible, but it isn't," I went on. "I loved them and they loved me too."

"Wow." He put his hands behind his head, staring up at the ceiling. "I had no idea."

"I didn't advertise it," I replied. I didn't remind him that he and I had been in the middle of getting divorced, either. "I think most people wouldn't understand."

He looked over at me. "Why are you telling me this now?"

Good question, I thought. I glanced at the door, hearing the water running in the sink, knowing Nico would be back soon.

"Because Carrie and Doc had a special relationship."

Mason rolled his eyes. "What's that supposed to mean?"

I had to make him understand.

"The Baumgartners were committed to each other, no matter what," I explained. "Bringing me into their marriage didn't change their love for each other. *Nothing* could change that. Don't you see?"

"No..." He frowned. "Go ahead, hit me over the head with it. What are you talking about?"

I swallowed and finally spit it out. "I think we're like that."

"Like the Baumgartners?"

"Yes!" I cried. The water had turned off in the bathroom. I expected Nico back any moment. "Look at what we've gone through. My God, we even got divorced, and still, I kept on loving you. I can't stop loving you, Mason. I never, ever will."

"I know." He smiled softly, brushing the hair away from my eyes. "Me too."

"I don't think it would matter what happened or who came into our lives, we would still love each other."

He nodded. "That's true."

"So... if we commit to each other, love each other... why can't we love someone else too?"

He looked at me and I saw the understanding in his eyes, finally. "Nico?"

I nodded, snuggling up against his chest, waiting. Waiting for him to explode with anger. Waiting for Nico to come in and break up our conversation. Waiting for the world to end. Or begin. Whichever came first.

"Why not?" he finally murmured. I lifted my head, looking at him, incredulous. "Dani, as long as I know you're mine, I could share you with anyone. The whole damned world could have you, as long as I knew you were coming back to me."

"That's how I feel too." I blinked back tears.

"I want you to be happy." He rubbed his thumb along my jaw line. "And clearly, Nico makes you happy."

"You make me happy too," I countered.

"I know." He smiled. "But Dani... I have to know you're mine."

"I am," I insisted. "I always will be."

"Then marry me."

It wasn't a question, but I answered it anyway, without hesitation.

"Yes."

He brightened. "Really?"

"Yes. Yes!" I threw my arms around him and this time I let my tears fall as we rolled around on the bed, laughing and crying at the same time.

"Forever this time?" he whispered in my ear.

"It was always forever," I said. "We just took a little break."

He kissed me, sealing the deal, as Nico came into the room. He stood there nude, framed in the doorway, looking at us.

"So I guess you've made your decision," he said, looking at me.

Oh God. How much had he heard?

"Yes," Mason replied, sitting up. I glanced at him, eyes wide. "And we'd like you to be a part of it, if you're willing."

"Come here." I sat too, reaching my hand out for Nico.

He came to the bed he shared with both of us, listening to what we proposed, and it *was* a proposal, of sorts. There would be no piece of paper between the three of us, no legal document, but he would be ours and we would be his.

And when he said yes, I sobbed with happiness, falling into his arms, into *both* of their arms. Nothing had ever felt so right.

Chapter Nine

Dear Carrie and Doc,

I made my decision. I made it before I even received your letter, but of course, you suggested the very thing I ultimately decided on. Go figure! I can't thank you enough for being courageous enough to tell me what to do. I know I was being crazy. I was crazy. Maybe I still am! But it takes quite a friend to shake another one awake and tell them... what was it? "Making choices means making commitments."

Yes, it does. And I've committed. Some people may say I need to be committed, but I've chosen what works for me, for us. Mason was and is and always will be my first love, just like Doc is yours. I can't deny that. But I love Nico too, and thankfully, so does Mason. And both of them love me. What could be more perfect than that?

I don't know what will happen in the future, what it may bring. Italy beckons and Nico's home and family are here, but Mason can't speak a word of Italian (although Nico is working hard on helping him learn!) and his parents, although he claims he's not their slave anymore, don't want him to stay here, and they've made that pretty unequivocally clear.

What happens if Mason and I move back to the states? Will Nico follow? What happens if I find a job in Italy? Will Mason be willing to stay? So much is up in the air.

But at least now I know. My choice is made. I have committed myself to this, and I have two men who love me beyond words. I am a very, very lucky woman.

"I told her we'd come by for half an hour or so." Nico squeezed my hand as we climbed the stairs to his mother's flat. I could hear Mama Dorotea calling to one of Nico's siblings, something about setting the table. "She wanted to do something nice for your graduation."

"Are you sure you guys want me tagging along?" Mason asked, standing behind us as we stopped at the door. "I don't think your mother likes me very much."

"I don't care." Nico's jaw tightened. "Besides, we won't stay long, I promise."

Everyone was already there, Nico's sisters busying themselves setting the table, except for the younger Caprice, who was holding the baby in her lap. He was smiling and laughing, almost sitting up by himself already. Anna's husband, Sal, and Giulia's husband, Will, were parked in front of the television, and Anna's two kids were on the floor playing a card game.

"There she is!" Mama Dorotea spoke in English, her accent thick. "The graduation girl!"

There was a big banner "CONGRATULATIONS DANIELLA" hanging on the wall. I didn't quibble about the spelling.

Mama Dorotea hugged me, rocking back and forth, patting me on the back, saying *"Congratulazioni!"* again and again. I thanked her, finally disengaging myself, only to have her turn her attentions to her son, hugging him even harder than she had me, crooning over him.

Mason watched this with a mixture of unease and amusement on his face. I took his hand and squeezed it, leading him into the room.

"Cute kid." Mason sat on the sofa, looking down at Caprice playing with Luka on the floor. "He's getting big."

"Want to hold him?" Caprice offered, lifting the baby up. I glanced over to see Mama Dorotea whispering something intently in Nico's ear.

"Ummm." Mason didn't have much choice. Caprice plopped the baby in his lap, standing and brushing off her jeans.

"I'll be right back," she said, heading down the hallway toward her room.

"Okay then." Mason lifted Luka up under the arms, looking at him. The baby drooled, giving us a toothless smile. God, it still made my uterus hurt to look at a baby, but it was different than before. Now it was the pain of wanting, instead of the pain of loss.

"You look good with a baby in your arms," I teased him.

He smiled over at me, letting the baby bounce on his knees.

"How's the heir to the throne?" Nico asked, joining us in the living room. Mama Dorotea had finally let him go and had busied herself instructing her daughters to rearrange place settings at the table.

"Drooling," Mason informed him, watching a dark spot growing on the thigh of his dress pants where a pool of Luka's saliva had fallen.

"He's teething," Giulia called from the dining room where I could see her folding napkins. "Breastfeeding is murder nowadays."

"Oh." Mason blinked. "I'm sorry to hear that."

"At least he's getting some," Will grumbled. He said it in Italian and Mason raised his eyebrows at me when I laughed.

"Tell you later," I whispered.

"So Daniella, what are you going to do now that you've graduated?" Anna asked, coming into the living room. She sat on the arm of the chair her husband was kicked back in. Everyone was speaking English for Mason's benefit.

I shrugged. "Look for a job, I guess."

"In Italy or back in the states?" Giulia joined her sister in the living room, reaching for the baby. Mason gave Luka back and I smiled at his reluctance.

"I'm not really sure..." I glanced at Mason and then at Nico.

"You have to hear this!" Caprice came into the room waving a CD case. "I'm in looooooove with this singer!"

Will and Sal protested but she put it on the stereo anyway, some American pop singer I'd never heard of named Rick Astley.

"Everything okay?" I leaned in so just Nico could hear me over the sound of the music.

He shrugged one shoulder, looking up as Mama Dorotea appeared in the doorway.

"Well, in honor of Daniella's graduation," she said, her accent heavy. "I have something to give to her."

Nico and I exchanged amused looks. She was talking like I wasn't even in the room.

"Girls, help me," she said, urging them to follow her.

"What in the world?" I mused, watching as Anna and Caprice followed their mother out the door. It wasn't long before I found out. All three of them reappeared in the doorway carrying a ton of cream-colored satin and lace.

Nico half-stood, his jaw dropped. I just stared, aghast, as all of them held up the dress, spreading the train out on the floor. It was the most beautiful dress I'd ever seen, and looking at Mama Dorotea's face, I knew I was going to have to break her heart.

"For you," she said proudly. "I made it myself. I can't wait for you to be my new daughter."

She was actually blinking back tears, which just made it worse, and brought tears to my own eyes.

"Nico," I whispered, gulping.

"Mama, you shouldn't have done this." He stood fully now, looking back at me. "I can't believe you did this."

"Well I know it's a little premature," she said by way of apology. "But your sister said you bought her a ring, and I know she's going to say yes."

Mama Dorotea beamed at me and I smiled weakly back, feeling sick. Then it dawned on me, exactly what she'd just said.

"You... what?" I blinked up at Nico. "A ring?"

He shrugged, reddening. "It was before... before I knew."

"Knew what?" Mama Dorotea demanded, arms crossed over her chest.

Mason cleared his throat, standing. "That Dani's agreed to marry me."

"Again?" Anna exclaimed.

"Yes," I replied. "Again."

Mama Dorotea drew herself up to her full height—all of about five-foot-two—and shook her finger at me. "How dare you come into my house! How dare you do this to my son!"

Nico stepped between her and me—she was heading straight for me, like a cat, claws out—grabbing her wrists. Everyone stared—even the baby had stopped fussing to watch.

"Mama, it's fine."

She frowned up at him. "What?"

"It's fine," he said again, letting her go, but not letting her get to me either. "I knew about it. Dani told me. She's made her decision and it's final."

"I'm sorry," I whispered, blinking back tears.

I felt Mason's hand on my shoulder. "Maybe we should go."

"No!" Nico turned to me, frowning. "I want you to stay."

I looked up at him, pleading with my eyes, and then he sighed.

"I'm sorry you went through all this work." I looked at the dress then at Mama Dorotea. "I'm so... so sorry."

"You should be." She glared at me around her son. "You're going to regret this!" Then she turned and stalked off toward the kitchen, leaving her daughters holding the dress.

"Let's go." Nico sighed.

Mama Dorotea reappeared in the doorway. "Where do you think you're going?"

"Home," he said, taking my hand. Mason already had my other one.

"Don't you walk out that door!" Mama Dorotea pulled at Nico's shirt as we started for the door. "Don't you dare!"

"Mama!" He spoke Italian back to her. "Listen to me. I'm a grown man. I've been old enough to make my own decisions for a long time. I love you, but I'm your child, not your possession. You don't own me.

You don't get to say where I go or what I do. Please. Just... let me go."

She stood in the doorway, tears streaming down her face, and I felt horrible for her in that moment. I wanted to put my arms around her and comfort her, but I knew I was the last person she wanted sympathy from.

She proved that at the last moment, calling, "He's far too good for you anyway!" before slamming the door behind us.

"Well," Mason said as we went down the stairs. "That was awful."

"She's just pouting," Nico replied, taking my hand again as we started to walk, Mason on my other side. "She'll get over it."

"But..." I swallowed, glancing up at Nico. "I have to know. Are you really okay with this?"

"I told you, it's just a piece of paper," he replied, swinging my hand. The day was bright and beautiful, the water of the canal dappled with afternoon sunshine. "I know you love me, and I don't care, as long as we're together."

"Let's go home," Mason said.

And that's just what we did.

Lunch with Cara Lucia went far better than I thought it would. She wasn't angry with me. In fact, she sounded truly happy when I told her that I was getting married again.

It was when I told her, a bit reluctantly, about Nico that she really surprised me.

"You are a very blessed woman," she said. "Not many women get to be Beatrice to one man's Dante— let alone two."

And she was right. Of course she was.

"I don't know... why me?" I wondered aloud, touching the necklace I always wore now—the emerald eye of Beatrice, who went to hell and was redeemed in the end.

"The real Beatrice was an inspiration to Dante Alighieri, the man," she reminded me. "She was his savior, the woman who saved him from himself."

I shrugged. "I don't think I'm saving anyone."

"Sure you are." Cara Lucia smiled and poured more tea. "Yourself."

I stormed into our flat, ready to tell both Mason and Nico the story of my job interview, which included a fat, old Italian man who looked down my blouse the whole time and put his hand on my knee and asked if I liked cream—*cream*, emphasized with waggling eyebrows and all—in my tea, but by the time I'd put my purse down and taken off my heels, I realized no one was home.

At least, that's what I thought at first.

I started back to our bedroom—we'd been sleeping in Mason's room, although it really belonged to all three of us now—when I saw the bathroom door was ajar. The shower was running.

Well, I decided, at least I could tell *someone* about my horrible interview.

I pushed the door open, ready to tell my story, when I heard Mason moan.

"Ahhh God, that's good," he groaned. "Where the hell did you learn to do that?"

Do what? I wondered. I stood still in the doorway, my head cocked, listening.

"It's not hard." That was Nico's voice. He was in the shower too.

"I beg to differ."

Nico chuckled. "You can try if you want."

Try...what? I crept closer, glancing at the mirror, so fogged with steam I couldn't see myself. How long had they been in there?

Now Nico was moaning.

"Yes, yes," he urged. "Oh that's good. Suck it!"

My jaw dropped and I took another step toward the shower, too curious for my own good. I probably should have just walked away, but I couldn't. The sound of them together made my heart pound and my ass clench. It was so hot I could have melted into a puddle right there on the bathroom floor.

"Fuck," Mason panted. "This makes my dick so hard."

And my pussy wet, I thought, my fingers reaching for the edge of the shower curtain. It was a light powder blue color to match the rugs—a hand-me-down from Nico's other sister, Giulia. I knew what I was going to see if I pulled that curtain aside, and yes, God yes, I did want to see it... but I was hesitant to let them know I was there.

"That's it," Nico encouraged. "Stroke that hard cock while you suck my dick. That's so good!"

I bit my lip, using one finger to pull the curtain, just an inch or two, enough so I could peek in. Mason was on his knees, Nico's cock buried in his mouth, his own cock a blur, his fist moving like lightning between his legs. The water poured down over Nico's shoulders and chest and belly. Thankfully, his eyes were closed, his head back, a hand on Mason's head, guiding him.

Mason's back was to me, and he was too busy to notice me standing there watching.

"Come here." Nico's eyes opened and I shrank back, but I couldn't stop watching. The two of them together like that was too compelling. Thankfully they didn't see me. Mason stood and the two men kissed, their tongues thrashing, the shower beating down on their wet heads. I watched Nico reach down and grab Mason's cock in his hand, tugging gently. Mason did the same to Nico, stroking nice and easy as they kissed.

"I'll let you fuck my ass if you want it," Nico whispered, hooking his leg around Mason, pulling him in close. I heard Mason moan, heard the lust in it, and I couldn't help lifting my skirt, nudging my panties aside so I could touch myself while I watched.

"I don't know if I'm ready for that..." Mason hesitated, running a hand through his hair, but the hand yanking on his cock looked like it was really beginning to change his mind.

"Whenever you want." Nico smiled, his eyes searching Mason's under the heat of the water, and that's when he saw me. I had my fingers in my panties, rubbing at my little clit, but he couldn't see any of that—just the top part of my head at the edge of the curtain. His eyebrows went up and he grinned. "Well, it looks like we have company."

I shrank back, swallowing hard, calling out, "I'm sorry. I just got back from my interview."

Mason peeked his head out, blinking and wiping water out of his eyes. "How did it go?"

"I didn't get the job." Telling them about the old, perverted Italian man seemed irrelevant now.

Mason grimaced. "I told you not to go. You were far too overqualified for that job."

"Poor bella." Nico was looking out at me over Mason's head. "Why don't you come in here and let us cheer you up?"

"Really?" I stood, hesitant. "I don't want to...interrupt."

"Get in here," Mason insisted, rolling his eyes.

I stripped down to nothing, leaving my skirt and blouse and stockings on the floor, joining them naked in the shower. Mason wrapped me in his arms, kissing me deeply, and Nico slid his arms around my waist from behind. I could feel the press of his cock against my ass, so very hard. They must have been playing for a long time. They were both full to bursting, cocks red and balls drawn tight.

"Are you mad?" Mason whispered, brushing a wet strand of hair from my face.

I looked at him, confused. "About what?"

He looked over at Nico and shrugged. "About... this? Us together?"

It took me a moment to realize what he meant. "Are you kidding me?" I grinned. "That was the hottest thing I've ever walked in on. And I just got invited to the party. I'm pretty sure I'm the luckiest woman on the planet."

Mason smiled, his hands roaming over my breasts. Nico was already cupping my mound from behind, his fingers working between the slippery lips of my pussy. I moaned and leaned back against Nico as his fingers slipped inside, fingering me gently. Mason thumbed my nipples and then leaned in to tongue them, the heat of the shower and my own lust making me dizzy.

"I want that pussy." Mason looked at Nico. "Hold her."

Nico grabbed me around the waist, lifting, and Mason squatted down, putting my legs over his shoulders, and then stood. I squealed, feeling my whole body rising into the air, Nico holding me from behind and Mason from the front, his face buried between my legs. The water was beating down on his head, spraying my belly and pussy, threatening to drown him, but he didn't let me go, his tongue thrashing against my clit, a ruthless storm.

Then he sank his fingers into me, the wet slosh of my pussy as he fucked me echoing against the tile. I cried out, straining and bucking in their arms, caught between the two of them, feeling my orgasm rising like a swell.

"Oh yes!" I cried, throwing my head back against Nico's shoulder, Mason's mouth fastened over my mound, relentless. "Oh I'm gonna come!"

The rapid pulse of my pussy around Mason's fingers told him that much. My climax was a rolling assault from every nerve in my body, shaking me to my core. Mason slowly lowered my limp body, but he didn't let me go. Instead, he wrapped my legs around his waist, aiming his cock for my center. Nico was nestled in behind me, and I remembered being like this that first time, when we all had taken a shower together. It felt like so long ago, a lifetime.

"I'm going to fuck her cunt." Mason met Nico's eyes as he slid his cock into my pussy. His next words sent a jolt through me. "You can have *her* ass for now... Maybe someday you can have mine."

I groaned, clinging to him, feeling his cock throbbing inside of me as Nico soaped up his cock, using it as lubricant. When I felt him pressing against my ass, I cried out, my teeth grazing Mason's shoulder. He held me still, holding my ass open and steady.

"Easy," Mason urged. "Oh God. I can feel your cock going into her ass..."

So could I. My nails dug into Mason's back, the stretch and burn between my legs almost too much to bear.

"Ohhh God oh God ohgodohgodohgod!" I gasped as Nico pressed his cock in deep, only a thin membrane separating his cock from Mason's inside of him.

"Oh she's so tight," Nico groaned, his hands on my ass too, both of them holding me up.

"Her pussy feels like a fifteen-year-old's," Mason gasped.

"So big," I managed to choke out, holding on for dear life as they both began to fuck me, filling me completely with their cocks.

"Are you all right?" Nico panted, but he didn't stop fucking my ass. "Oh God, bella, your fucking ass is so good!"

"Yes!" I turned my head, kissing him, sucking at his tongue. "It's good! Oh yes! So good!"

Mason groaned and his fingers dug into my ass, leaving instant bruises. "Fuck! Fuck! Gonna come!"

They were both raising and lowering me on their dicks in rhythm, thrusting up hard.

Nico broke our kiss to cry out, "Me too! Oh God! I'm going to fill your little asshole!"

And then they were both bombarding me with cum, fucking me with brutal, primal lust, all thought gone. I felt each pulsing swell of their cocks together inside of me, emptying themselves with astonishing force. I just hung on and whimpered until it was over and they slowly pulled out, lowering my feet to the tub floor and sandwiching me between them with kisses.

Then we actually showered, washing our own bodies and each other's, teasing and playful, slowly coming back to some semblance of reality. They both got out first, toweling off, while I washed my hair. By the time I joined them in the bedroom, they were already getting dressed.

"I'm hungry," I complained. I'd been too nervous to eat before the interview. Now I was starving.

"You're always hungry." Nico buttoned his jeans, reaching for a shirt.

I perked up. "Are you cooking?"

"I thought we'd go out to dinner," Mason suggested. "Down in the Piazza."

"Where?" Nico frowned. He was so picky about where he would eat. "The tourists are coming back. I don't want to go anywhere trendy."

Mason smiled. "It's a surprise."

So we went.

The sun was high and bright. The weather had shifted from spring to early summer, the shade of the canopy on the water-bus a welcome relief from the sun, a breeze off the water cooling my skin as I sat between the two of them, holding each of their hands. I saw a blond woman looking at us curiously. She'd noticed Mason getting on, helping me in, and then I'd seen her looking appreciatively at Nico as well.

They're mine, I thought, hiding a secret smile. I could hardly believe it myself.

"So where is this surprise?" Nico followed Mason through the crowds in the Piazza and I tagged along behind. Tourist season was in full swing, vendors at every corner of the square, people crowded on benches, standing together and smiling, taking pictures near the statues.

Mason halted abruptly and Nico managed to stop, but I didn't. It was like running into a wall.

"There's nothing here." Nico stated the obvious.

Shops and restaurants lined the square, but we'd stopped in front of an empty building, a sign in the window: *Vendita.*

For sale.

"How do you like our new restaurant?" Mason was trying to hide a smile.

My jaw dropped. "What did you do?"

"Instead of investing my money in my father's franchise, I thought I'd invest it here." Mason turned to Nico. "And of course, I'll need a good local chef."

"You're kidding me?" Nico said in English, turning to look at the front of the restaurant. It was in the old part of the Piazza, the architecture traditional, beautiful high arches and decorative scrollwork.

"What shall we call it?" Mason asked, pulling a key out of his pocket and opening the door. Inside was even more beautiful that out.

"How about Dani's?" Nico offered, putting an arm around my waist.

I looked at Mason with tears in my eyes, overwhelmed with his generosity. "How about Bella's?"

"Beautiful," he said, and it was.

Mason turned to me, slipping his arm around my waist too. "You know, I'm also going to need a hostess. Someone to run the front of the restaurant. Someone who speaks fluent Italian..."

I grinned up at him. "I may know someone who could fill that position for you."

"I thought you might." Mason kissed the top of my head.

"Bella's," Nico said softly, glancing down at me. "It's perfect."

And it was.

Epilogue

Dear Carrie and Doc,

We did it. I walked down the aisle wearing the dress Mama Dorotea made for me. (She finally forgave us, although she still doesn't quite understand our "arrangement!") Picture (and I'm enclosing many of them!) me walking down the aisle, Mason dressed in a tux, and Nico right beside him, his best man.

They're both my best men.

I'm so sorry Janie got so sick and you couldn't make it! We were all looking forward to seeing you. My mother didn't make it either, if it makes you feel any better, and she didn't have anywhere near as good an excuse. She never wanted me to come to Italy in the first place, and I'm sure she isn't happy that I'm staying. But I'm happy. So very happy. I'm wearing two rings now, one on each hand.

I don't have to tell you how amazing the honeymoon was. We decided not to go anywhere at all. What's better than Venice in the summer?

Gianni Bonaccorsi catered the wedding for us for free. He was so thrilled when we opened Bella's, said he welcomed the competition from anyone as talented as Nico. So now Mason is handling the business side of our new restaurant venture, Nico is cooking, and I'm running the front of the restaurant. It's perfection.

And if that wasn't enough, I have even more amazing news...

I fantasized planning some amazing, romantic way to tell them, but when it came right down to it, the minute I found out, I just couldn't wait.

I was out of breath already, but I ran into *Bella's*, past the hostess we'd hired to give me a little break once in a while, winding my way through the maze of tables to the back of the restaurant.

Nico was in the middle of poaching eggs and I dragged him into Mason's office while he called to his sous chef, "Watch the salmon!"

"Well, hi there." Mason glanced up at the two of us, Nico's chef hat askew, my face flushed. "What's up?"

I just blurted it out. "I'm pregnant."

Both men stared at me in disbelief. Nico turned to me, jaw dropped. Mason stood, holding onto the edge of his desk.

"Whose...?" Nico looked at me, then at Mason.

"Whose is it?" Mason echoed.

I laughed, my hands on my hips. "Does it really matter?"

Then they were both pulling me into their arms, and we laughed and cried and hugged.

It didn't matter. We were together. We were going to be a real family.

And that was all that really mattered.

ABOUT SELENA KITT

Selena Kitt is a NEW YORK TIMES bestselling and award-winning author of erotica and erotic romance fiction. She is one of the highest selling erotic writers in the business with over a million books sold!

Her writing embodies everything from the spicy to the scandalous, but watch out-this kitty also has sharp claws and her stories often include intriguing edges and twists that take readers to new, thought-provoking depths.

When she's not pawing away at her keyboard, Selena runs an innovative publishing company (excessica.com) and book store (www.excitica.com).

Her books EcoErotica (2009), The Real Mother Goose (2010) and Heidi and the Kaiser (2011) were all Epic Award Finalists. Her only gay male romance, Second Chance, won the Epic Award in Erotica in 2011. Her story, Connections, was one of the runners-up for the 2006 Rauxa Prize, given annually to an erotic short story of "exceptional literary quality."

She can be reached on her website at
www.selenakitt.com

YOU'VE REACHED

"THE END!"

Made in the USA
Middletown, DE
27 May 2015